"You
do you know that?"

Gabe shook his head in disgust, then lightly touched his index finger to the center of her chest. "What makes you tick, Ms. Fletcher? Surely there can't be a heart in there."

Erica ignored this gibe just as she was sure she would have to overlook much of what Gabriel Logan would say in the weeks to come. "My conditions are simple," she told him. "One, my duties in this house will involve only Amanda, and two, you keep your distance."

"All right," he said at last, holding out his hand. "Your duties will be limited to caring for Amanda." As Erica put her pale hand in his tan one, he added thoughtfully, "But I have to see for myself whether or not the second condition is necessary."

Before Erica could draw away, Gabe pulled her none too gently against his chest and lifted her chin so that his mouth could capture hers.

Dear Reader,

It's that time of year again—pink hearts, red roses and sweet dreams abound as we celebrate that most amorous of holidays—St. Valentine's Day!

Silhouette Romance captures the sentimental mood of the month with six new tales of lovers who are meant for each other—and even if *they* don't realize it from the start, *you* will!

Last month, we launched our new FABULOUS FATHERS series with the first heartwarming tale of fatherhood. Now, we bring you the second title in the series, *Uncle Daddy*. Popular author Kasey Michaels has packed this story with humor and emotion as hero Gabe Logan learns to be a father—and a husband.

Also in February, Elizabeth August's *The Virgin Wife* whisks you away to Smytheshire, a fictional town where something dark and secret is going on. Once you've been there, you'll want to visit this wonderful, intriguing place again—and you can! Be sure to look for other Smytheshire books coming in the near future from Elizabeth August and Silhouette Romance.

To complete this month's offerings, we have book one of Laurie Paige's new ALL-AMERICAN SWEETHEARTS series, *Cara's Beloved*, as well as *To the Rescue* by Kristina Logan, *Headed for Trouble* by Joan Smith and Marie Ferrarella's *Babies on His Mind*.

In months to come, we'll be bringing you books by all your favorite authors—Diana Palmer, Annette Broadrick, Suzanne Carey and more! In the meantime, we at Silhouette Romance wish you a Happy Valentine's Day spent with someone special!

Anne Canadeo
Senior Editor

UNCLE DADDY
Kasey Michaels

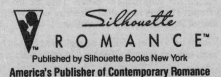

Silhouette
R O M A N C E™
Published by Silhouette Books New York
America's Publisher of Contemporary Romance

For Adam, my first grandchild, who reminded me
how gloriously wonderful babies are.

SILHOUETTE BOOKS
300 E. 42nd St., New York, N.Y. 10017

UNCLE DADDY

ISBN: 0-373-08916-3

First Silhouette Books printing February 1993

All the characters in this book have no existence outside the
imagination of the author and have no relation whatsoever to
anyone bearing the same name or names. They are not even
distantly inspired by any individual known or unknown to the
author, and all incidents are pure invention.

Printed in the U.S.A.

Books by Kasey Michaels

Silhouette Romance

Maggie's Miscellany #331
Compliments of the Groom #542
Popcorn and Kisses #572
To Marry at Christmas #616
His Chariot Awaits #701
Romeo in the Rain #743
Lion on the Prowl #808
Sydney's Folly #834
Prenuptial Agreement #898
Uncle Daddy #916

KASEY MICHAELS,

the author of more than two dozen books, divides her creative time between Silhouette Romance and Regency novels. Married and the mother of four, Kasey's writing has garnered the Romance Writers of America Golden Medallion Award and the *Romantic Times* Best Regency Trophy.

Fabulous Fathers

Gabe Logan On Fatherhood...

How can I explain what it feels like to realize that you'd be willing to give up everything you have, and everything you could ever hope to have, for a small scrap of humanity who doesn't even have any teeth? I don't think I can. I mean, have you ever seen a newborn baby? They all look like my old geography teacher, Mr. Higgenbottom—bald, toothless and totally incapable of coherent speech!

And yet, when I first saw Amanda, my brother's orphaned infant, I was lost. Completely, totally lost. Me, a bachelor, a man who hadn't even thought about marriage, let alone raising a baby on my own—and a baby girl at that!

But I took that first look at Mandy, and I was a goner. I knew that Mandy was mine, and that I'd do anything for her.

And you know what? I'm a good father. A *damn* good father—Mandy's "Uncle Daddy."

Who would have believed it? Not me.

Chapter One

Gabe Logan frowned, unconsciously lifting a hand to stroke his mustache. She was out there again, just as she had been for the past two days. "If I didn't know better," he muttered under his breath, "I'd think she was casing the joint."

Allowing the vertical blinds to glide back into place, Gabe stepped away from the window and its view of the dark blue sports car parked at a discreet distance from his sprawling suburban ranch house. He rubbed at the back of his neck. For days he'd suffered from the vague, prickling feeling that someone was watching him. Now he knew for sure that it hadn't just been his imagination.

She had been in Trexler Park the day he had taken Mandy there to play on a blanket while he sketched.

She had been haphazardly filling a shopping cart with a half dozen bottles of catsup as he and Mandy did the weekly marketing at the local supermarket.

She had even been seated in the last pew at church this past Sunday, her face barely visible beneath a large-brimmed straw hat.

The tallish, too slim blonde reeked of money and breeding, and she looked as out of place in the park, the grocery store and the small church as an orchid would look stuck in a marigold patch.

Perhaps that was why Gabe had noticed her. His artistic eye had been drawn to her fine, patrician features, the pale gold of her overly neat hair. He had felt the urge to go up to her and pull the pins from her hair, even as he reminded himself of his newly acquired aversion to beautiful blondes.

At first it had seemed coincidental. Then he had made a little game out of watching for her to appear like a rabbit out of a hat every time he turned around.

But now she had overplayed her hand. Three days' worth of seeing that same sports car parked at the curb had all but exhausted his sense of humor. Rock stars had trouble with groupies. Or actors. Even his brother, Gary, had met with his share of ardent fans. But not Gabe Logan. Not a lowly biology textbook illustrator.

He closed his eyes, his decision made. He'd wait until it was dark, until Mandy had fallen asleep. He'd wait, while the blonde kept her damned vigil as she had done for the past two nights. He'd wait—and then he'd act.

Several lights burned inside the house, evidence that its inhabitants were still up and about. By now she had decided which of the two small wings held the bedrooms, not that she knew what she could possibly do with that knowledge.

Why hadn't she simply hired a private detective to handle this end of things? *Because this is too important,* she thought, shaking her head. *This situation is too delicate, too potentially explosive to trust to anyone else.*

Erica Fletcher still couldn't believe, couldn't make her mind accept the startling facts that had led her to this quiet Allentown suburb.

Was it only a week earlier, a full month after Meredith's death, that she had hidden in her bedroom, gathering the courage needed to perform the difficult task of going through her sister's personal belongings?

A lone car wended its way down the hill toward her, its headlights picking out her finely sculpted features before passing on down the street. As she stared into the rearview mirror, watching the taillights disappear into the darkness, her mind traveled back to that last fateful day. The world outside her car disappeared, and once again she was standing in her bedroom, experiencing all the nervousness, all the unremitting dread, that she had felt at the time.

It was something she had to face; heaven only knew she had put it off too long. Mrs. James had offered, but Erica knew it was not a job for a housekeeper, no matter how dedicated. This was a task only Meredith's sole remaining relative could do.

Meredith had been the baby of the family, the beautiful, dimpled blond cherub who could break hearts with her smile. She didn't have to play a musical instrument or excel at her schoolwork to gain their parents' attention. She just had to be her appealing, outgoing self to have everyone she met eating out of her hand.

It had been different for Erica. Five years Meredith's senior, with her horn-rimmed glasses constantly slipping off her nose, her own fair tresses pulled back severely into a tight no-nonsense ponytail, Erica had always been the serious sister. The "smart" sister. The "plain" sister. The "overachiever."

Henry and Blair Fletcher had loved both of their daughters in their own offhand way, but it had always been easier to love Meredith.

After the death of their parents, Meredith had left her exclusive finishing school over Erica's protests. Like an exotic butterfly, Meredith had flitted gaily about—the entire world suddenly at her disposal.

And she'd loved it all, Erica remembered with a sad smile. Poor, flighty Meredith. Her violent end, met beneath the devastating force of an alpine avalanche, had seemed such a cruel contradiction to her whimsical, cotton-candy life.

Erica sighed. Her sister's death had been tragic and difficult to accept. But at last she had summoned the courage to deal with its remnants. She recalled how she had finally directed her steps down the hallway toward Meredith's bedroom, the room in which her sister had dreamed so many dreams that no longer had any chance of becoming reality.

Erica remembered how she had stepped hesitantly, silently, onto the deep, plush white carpet spread before her like a soft mantle of snow—she shook her head ruefully at the comparison—and had cast her gaze around Meredith's pink and white room.

The room was unchanged, a fluffy, impractical confection full of slender French country furniture, gleaming satin and soft, flowing lace. Strange, Erica had thought at the time, how someone could be on this earth for a quarter century and leave nothing more substantial behind than a fairy-tale-princess boudoir and the lingering scent of French perfume.

But Meredith had left more than memories of her youthful, laughing beauty. She'd also left behind something infinitely less memorable—a sordid, tawdry scandal—and Erica was still reeling from the shock of it.

How could Meredith, that willful but never evil child of Erica's memory, have run off to Europe with a married man? Yet Meredith had done just that. Hotel reservations did not lie—not to mention the fact that her lover had perished with her beneath the snows.

The European and American tabloids had enjoyed a field day with the news, not caring whom they hurt in their search for a titillating story.

Erica's clear green eyes took on a hard glitter. Even now, she could feel the anger that had risen inside her; anger directed almost equally at the reporters and at the philandering husband who had hypnotized her gullible sister. Meredith had been a victim, not the vile seductress the press had painted her.

Then why, a niggling voice inside her nudged, *why did it take you so long to find the courage to go through Meredith's personal papers? What were you afraid you'd find that day in her bedroom—a diary crammed with descriptions of wild parties and one-night flings?*

"Ah, Erica," she murmured tiredly into the warm summer night as she lowered her forehead to rest it against the soft leather covering of the steering wheel.

"Don't you only wish it could have been that simple?"

The hand that reached through the open window to grab Erica's shoulder was decidedly masculine in its strength. It pushed her forward, so that she was unable to turn to see her attacker.

"All right, sweetheart, don't move," came a deep male voice doing a very bad Humphrey Bogart impression. "I'm Gabe Logan, chief of the Neighborhood Watch. You and me's got some talking to do. Now—do we do this easy or do we do this hard?"

Erica swallowed with a small gulp, glad she hadn't cried out in that first split second of panic. "We don't do this at all, Bogie," she muttered disgustedly into the steering wheel, sure that the man she had been stalking had somehow succeeded in turning the tables on her.

"What?" Gabriel Logan questioned, obviously startled. "You're not playing fair, lady. You're not following the script. You're supposed to be frightened—shaking in your boots."

"Sorry to disappoint you. But you'll have these little failures now and then," she sniped, the last of her fear giving way to anger. "Now why don't you take your grimy paw and your two-bit impression for a hike."

"Or else?" Gabe asked slowly.

"Or else I scream my head off. I'll have every neighbor on the block out here before you can blink."

The pressure of his hand eased slightly, just enough for her to straighten her spine and turn her head. She stared up at a grinning face, laughing blue eyes and a mustache that somehow had the name Tom Selleck popping, unwanted, into her head.

"Lady, didn't anyone ever tell you it's not wise to antagonize a dangerous man?"

Erica pointedly removed his fingers from her bare arm and remarked, "I'll remember that if I should ever happen to come across one. Humphrey Bogart? Give me a break!"

Gabe's face assumed a hurt expression. "I do a lot better with Donald Duck, but I didn't think it would sound quite as menacing."

"Good thought," Erica replied, reaching for the ignition so that she could activate the power windows. Her years spent in the cutthroat import-export business, dealing daily with men of every ilk, had given her more than a little confidence in her judgment of character. She had already decided that Gabriel Logan was what the world would call "a nice man." But it still unnerved her to realize that he had somehow gotten the advantage over her on this, their first meeting.

"Oh, no, you don't," he admonished, reaching in to jerk the keys from the ignition. "You've been following me, lady. And much as I'm flattered by all this attention, I think you owe me an explanation."

"Give me back my keys, Mr. Logan," Erica said coolly. "The Neanderthal pose doesn't suit you."

Gabe flashed her a grin. "Nothing I do seems to suit you, does it? So, what is it about me that attracts you? Or are you really a thief?"

"Don't be ridiculous," Erica bit out, rapidly losing her temper.

"Don't be ridiculous? *Me?*" Gabe asked. "You're sitting out here in the dark like a cat burglar, waiting till the coast is clear, and *I'm* ridiculous? Just when did you escape from the home?"

Obviously he wasn't going to give back her keys until she gave him a few answers. "All right, Mr. Logan. I do have a business matter to discuss with you," Erica gritted through clenched teeth, giving in to the inevitable.

"Lady, you sure have a strange way of doing business. Now, fun's fun and all that, but I can't stay out here all night. Why don't we get this show on the road? For starters, who the hell are you?" Gabe's voice still held a lingering edge of amusement.

"My name is Fletcher, Mr. Logan," Erica offered, striving to put this ridiculous situation onto a more serious footing. "Erica Fletcher."

"Fletcher?" Gabe barked, zeroing in on Erica's name. "Did you say *Fletcher?*"

What is the matter with this man? Erica wondered. She couldn't help but notice Gabe's suddenly white face and narrowed eyes. Anyone would think he'd just seen a ghost. "Yes, Fletcher. F-l-e-t—*Hey!*"

Before she knew what was happening, the car door was jerked open and she was being hauled unceremoniously to her feet. In the space of a heartbeat she was brought face-to-face with what could only be described as one very intimidating man.

"You even have the look of her, now that I can see you up close. Where is she? Never mind, don't answer that. I should be doing handsprings that she's not here. If there's any justice, she's burning in hell."

"Let go of me!" Erica ordered, trying to catch her breath.

"No way, lady. Not until I get some answers!" His fingers locked over her upper arms like solid bands.

"Now we're just going to go inside and have a nice, friendly little chat." His voice was deceptively soft, like velvet over ice, and Erica cringed at the underlying menace.

Without another word he turned and began to lead her across the yard toward the house.

Her pencil-thin heels sank deeply into the soft ground with every awkward step, her slim skirt forcing her to take two steps to his every one. Disheveled, and once again out of breath, Erica Wilburn Fletcher half stumbled through the open French doors.

Still holding tightly on to her bare left arm, Gabe lost no time in pushing her down into a soft, cushioned leather couch that proceeded to envelop her like some overgrown Venus's-flytrap.

"Are you crazy?" she shrieked, pushing back an errant lock of blond hair that had escaped its pins. Never in her twenty-eight years had she been treated so forcefully. "This is an outrage!"

"Wrong again. This is my house, the one you've been casing all week. And stay where you are," he added as Erica struggled to rise. "I have to go check on the baby. Can I trust a Fletcher to stay put for a minute or do I have to drag you along with me?"

The baby. Erica took a deep, shuddering breath. On a scale of one to ten, Erica liked Gabe's Humphrey Bogart voice much better than the hard-clipped tones he was employing now. If this was a nice man, it was a nice man whose best impression was a convincing revival of Dr. Jekyll and Mr. Hyde. And right now the intensity of his emotion scared her. She'd see the child soon enough, and without Gabriel Logan hovering over her, frightening her. "I—I'll stay right here," she stammered, avoiding his eyes.

"Smart choice." Just as she thought he was about to leave the room, giving her a few moments to regain her equilibrium, he stopped and asked, "Aren't you even going to ask to see her?"

So he did know why she was here. He wasn't quite as thick as she'd thought. She decided to play dumb— not that this overbearing man would notice. "See whom?"

"*Whom?* Aren't we just *too-too? Whom* do you think, Ms. Fletcher?" he countered sarcastically. "I mean Mandy, of course. Amanda Logan, age three months. Daughter of the delinquent Meredith Fletcher and the late Gary Logan. That is why you're here, isn't it? To see Mandy?"

"No, Mr. Logan," Erica replied stonily, carefully adjusting her skirt over her knees. The time had come to stop playing games. "I'm not here to *see* my sister's child. I'm here to take her *home*—to Philadelphia."

"Oh, yeah? You and whose army?" Gabe growled angrily. When she failed to answer, he turned and stalked out, his parting taunt replaying itself over and over in her ears.

Struggling to compose herself, Erica shifted against the cushions of the sofa. She regretted the fact that her well-equipped purse was left behind in her car. If she ever needed some feminine war paint, now was the time. But not one to waste time wishing for the impossible, she soon abandoned that idea and made a conscious effort to inventory the room in the hopes of learning more about Gabriel Logan, her adversary.

She was seated in a den, or family room, as she imagined such retreats were dubbed in the suburbs. An immense large-screen television dominated the entire room. With a curl of her upper lip, Erica scrutinized the high-tech monitor, mentally lowering Gabriel Logan a notch or two in her estimation.

Besides, she remembered, he had a mustache. Erica loathed mustaches.

At least he knows how to read, she thought nastily, continuing her inventory. Hundreds of books were jammed haphazardly into several floor-to-ceiling bookcases, volumes ranging from thick art histories to popular fiction. An obviously expensive stereo system took up the major part of another wall.

On the floor, in the midst of all this manly clutter, sat a pink plastic infant seat, a small cotton blanket, and an empty baby bottle. The room smelled of sardines and baby powder—an odd combination. Erica wrinkled her nose in distaste.

"Not exactly mainline, is it?" Gabe quipped, walking back into the room and sweeping a week's worth of newspapers from an ottoman to sit down directly in front of her. The baby, Meredith's child, wasn't with him. Erica bit back an inquiry as to whether the child was all right. "You did say Philadelphia, didn't you? I don't imagine you meant the inner city. And Mandy's fine, now that you ask."

"I'm not here to trade insults, Mr. Logan," Erica pointed out quietly, disappointed that he hadn't brought Amanda back to the den with him.

Gabe shook his head, chuckling slightly. "Really? You could have fooled me."

"Without even trying," Erica agreed sweetly, unable to hold her tongue. She sat up as straight as possible on the soft couch. "I suggest we get right to the point. You mentioned that your brother, Gary, is deceased. Meredith is also...dead."

"Is that so?" Gabe leaned back on the ottoman, lacing his fingers together over one raised knee. "Pardon me if I don't appear grief stricken."

Erica longed to hit him. "My only sister is gone. You may not have liked Meredith, Mr. Logan, which you have already made abundantly clear to me," she bit out tersely, "but you might at least have enough grace to consider showing a little respect for the dead."

"Is that right? Well, don't hold your breath, lady." Gabe fairly sneered the words. "Your sister led my brother on a merry chase and then dumped Mandy in his lap and disappeared, leaving behind some corny letter about the two of them cherishing their memories because there was no future for them. There sure as hell wasn't. Gary raced out of here like a madman, got himself roaring drunk, and ran his car into a tree. Ever spent three days watching your only brother die? Don't tell me about your precious sister!"

Oh, Meredith, Erica cried silently, hanging her head, *what a great deal of hurt you've left behind.* "I—I didn't know," she began softly. "I was away in Europe, then the Far East, on business, for over eight months. When I was contacted about Meredith's death, I had no idea she had been involved with anyone. I found the birth certificate only when I went through her personal papers last week."

"And that makes it all right?" Gabe asked sarcastically. "You know, I took one look at her and recognized her for what she was. But, Gary, the poor fool, was so infatuated with her pretty face—that pretty, lying, scheming face—that he wouldn't listen to me. Oh, no. He goes off to play house in Philadelphia, leaving his friends, his business—and then comes

home with his tail between his legs and his motherless
infant in his arms.''

Their conversation was going from bad to worse as
each new piece of information damned Meredith more
than the last. But Erica had to know it all. ''Ho-how
old was Amanda when Meredith ran away?''

''Three days. She left her all but abandoned in the
hospital. Some maternal instinct, huh?''

*Three days! Oh, that poor baby, left all alone like
that!* It sounded just like the sort of juvenile thing
Meredith would do. So childlike herself, Meredith was
hardly ready to raise an infant. *Why didn't she come
to me for help?* Even as she wondered, Erica shook her
head in dismissal. Meredith hadn't confided in her for
years. As different as night and day, the sisters hadn't
been close.

''What's past is past,'' Gabe said, cutting into the
silence. ''Mandy Logan is the present.''

''On the contrary, Mr. Logan. Amanda *Fletcher* is
the present,'' Erica countered swiftly, banishing her
thoughts of Meredith to concentrate on her niece.
''Although Gary Logan may be listed on the birth
certificate as her natural father, Amanda is very much
a Fletcher. One of the Philadelphia Fletchers, of F and
W Import-Export.''

Gabe leaned back, his hands still linked around one
bent knee. His long, lean body covered the ottoman
while his other leg stretched out nearly to the couch.
''Ah, yes. Now I remember. Good old F and W, long
may it reign. And you must be the wonder woman
who has taken over the family business. My, my, my.
Do I genuflect now, or should I just kiss your ring?''

Erica clumsily scrambled to her feet. How dare he
insult her? F and W was her life—she had *made* it her

life! Yet he made it—all her hard work—sound dirty, even petty. "You know something, Mr. Logan?" she offered, glaring down at him. "You're beginning to be a first-class pain in the—"

"Ms. Fletcher!" Gabe sat up straight, his eyebrows raised in exaggerated astonishment as he looked at her. "I didn't know they talked like that in high society! You could be tossed out of the social register. Just like I'm going to toss you out on your pretty little rear right now." His words gained impact as he rose, towering over her like a leering vulture.

"But we aren't quite finished with our discussion, Mr. Logan," Erica protested, even while backing away from him toward the French doors—and safety. She shouldn't have allowed her temper to get the better of her. She hadn't become so successful without knowing what it meant to be a cool-headed negotiator. "You haven't even heard my offer."

Gabe stopped in his tracks, his blue eyes mere slits in his lean, chiseled face. "Offer? What offer?"

"My offer to take Amanda off your hands, of course. Be reasonable, Mr. Logan. You're a bachelor. Surely a young baby must cramp a single man's life-style—not to mention your financial resources. You see . . . I've done my homework on you. Amanda is entitled to be raised amid the comfort her mother's share of F and W will provide. Meredith's child deserves the opportunities and advantages of the Fletcher family." She hoped her smile was ingratiating. "You can name your own price."

When Gabe didn't speak, Erica took a step toward the door. "If you'll excuse me while I go to the car and get my checkbook, I'm sure we can work this out to both our satisfactions. I'll allow Amanda to stay here

for the remainder of the night and you can say goodbye to her in the morning.''

She looked back at him, to gauge his response, and
immediately knew that she had blundered. She had
made her offer seem too cut and dried. She slanted a
look toward the door, still hoping the sight of her open
checkbook would make a better impression on him.
She'd meet his price. She'd meet any price. She had to
have Amanda!

As his shock at her cold, businesslike solution to
their "problem" faded away, a new emotion came into
his face. Anger. Deep, intense anger. Erica opened her
mouth to speak again just as Gabe sprang to action.
He grabbed her by the arm and growled, "Don't
bother. Mandy isn't for sale.''

A deep silence pervaded the room as the two com-
batants stared at each other. Her arms burned where
his fingertips gripped her flesh. Her heart pounded
painfully in her chest. All her "homework" had gone
for nothing. She had read her man wrong.

With a supreme effort of will, Erica counted very
deliberately to ten, and then to ten once again, before
speaking, laying all her cards on the bargaining table.
"Mr. Logan, I'm not going home without that baby.''

"Oh, you're cool, Philadelphia, I'll give you that,''
Gabe complimented with heavy sarcasm as he dropped
his hand, as if suddenly aware that he could be hurting her. "If anyone ever does the story of your life I'd
suggest they look for a young Grace Kelly type to play
the lead.''

He cocked his head to one side, listening, although
Erica hadn't heard anything. "Damn, there she goes
again. She's not used to hearing voices at night, I
guess. You stay here. Stay right here.''

Once Gabe was gone, Erica sank gratefully back onto the too soft couch and took several deep, steadying breaths. Obviously she had underestimated the man. Oh, certainly, he put on a great show of devotion to his niece, but Erica had been around long enough to face facts and discount dramatic outbursts.

Every man had his price; she had merely erred in her basic approach. All right, she conceded, mentally reworking her schedule, she would play it his way. First she'd listen to how much he "loved little Mandy"— surely a ploy meant to up the ante a bit—but the end result would be the same. She took another look at the large-screen television and allowed a smile to sneak onto her face.

"Sorry about that. She lost her pacifier," Gabe said as he reentered the room and sat on the ottoman once more. "Now, tell me. Whose turn is it to hurl the next insult? I've lost count."

Erica ignored his question. "Have you had Amanda ever since your brother died?"

Gabe nodded.

"You care for her all by yourself, without any help?"

Gabe smiled. "What can I say? It turns out Mary Poppins has an unlisted phone number."

Erica moved in for the kill. "And you allowed it to slip your mind that Meredith Fletcher of F and W Import-Export was Amanda's mother—just as you claim to be ignorant of Meredith's death? You'll pardon me if I find that rather hard to believe, considering that Meredith's picture was on the cover of nearly every tabloid in the country when she, um, when she died. Amanda is a considerable heiress."

There, it was out, the fact that she knew he was merely playing her for a sky-high settlement. The question was why had he waited for *her* to come to *him?* Most men would have broken down her door in their haste to introduce themselves once they had realized what a gold mine they'd stumbled into. Besides, he was an artist. Artists hardly ever made any *real* money until after they were dead—which Gabriel Logan might be real soon if he didn't stop baiting her!

Gabe's tone was terse, with all trace of humor gone. "Of course I knew who Meredith was. She told us, repeatedly. She was very proud of her connections."

Erica smiled, satisfied. "So you admit you knew that Meredith was quite wealthy."

Gabe slapped at his forehead with the flat of his hand. "Ah, comes the dawn! Stupid, Logan, real stupid. The lady wants to know if you're smart enough to realize that Mandy—at the tender age of three months—could buy and sell you forty times over. Maybe I should buy her some fourteen-karat-gold diaper pins?"

"You're overacting again, Mr. Logan," Erica pointed out, raising her chin slightly.

Gabe turned to glare at her, his eyes narrowed. "Tell me, Ms. Fletcher," he asked after a short, uncomfortable silence, "when you cut yourself, do you bleed green? Lady, I can see the dollar signs flashing in your eyes." Gabe got up and began pacing the room, obviously unable to sit still.

"I don't know why you're so touchy, Mr. Logan," Erica lied, knowing she'd hit a nerve. "I was merely leading up to the fact that it was rather hard *not* to know about Meredith's death."

Gabe stopped pacing and turned to face her, his expression bleak. "Much as this may surprise you, Ms. Fletcher, a man doesn't find a hell of a lot of time for casual reading when he's burying his brother and learning how to care for a helpless infant. Pardon me if reading about the latest jet-set doings didn't hit the top of my to-do list."

"Oh, yes, of course," Erica agreed in haste, suddenly ashamed of herself, and sorry for Gabriel Logan.

Neither feeling lasted long as Gabe spoke again. "What did dear Meredith do anyway—run into somebody's angry wife?"

Erica refused to rise to his bait this time. Instead she took a good look at Gabriel Logan, possibly her first unbiased assessment. He was definitely handsome. But was he being honest with her? Was *any* thirty-some-year-old bachelor so willing to give twenty years of his life to raising an infant niece?

"All right, Mr. Logan, we'll drop the money angle for the time being. But what about the responsibility?" she prodded sympathetically, tilting her head slightly as she looked at him. "Doesn't Amanda put a crimp in your, er, your social engagements?"

Gabe sneered, obviously not believing her show of concern for his love life. "I'm a man of moderation, Ms. Fletcher. Besides, you have no idea the number of sweet young things who nearly jump at the chance to help me with Mandy. Seems a man with a baby is seen as quite the romantic figure these days. Any other questions?" he asked, raising one finely shaped eyebrow in mock inquiry.

Erica twisted her full mouth into a thoughtful pout as she mentally shifted gears. "But your work...surely caring for a baby takes up much of your time?"

"I work at home, so my schedule is pretty much my own. Now, is there anything else, or are we about to go back to square one?"

"Square one?" Erica repeated.

"Yes, Ms. Fletcher," Gabe informed her, his tone hard. "You remember. Square one—all the way back to the part where you offer me money and I toss you out on your wallet."

Chapter Two

Erica wearily ran a hand across her forehead. She was getting a headache. This man wasn't playing by the rules, damn it. Having emerged the victor in dozens of boardroom battles during the past eight years, she found it frustrating to be suddenly dealing with a man who insisted on being so distressingly candid.

They were supposed to dance around each other a bit, chip away at one another, gaining ground here while allowing a few niggling concessions there, until the main objective was secured. But this man wasn't interested in pros and cons, or any sort of balance sheet that clearly demonstrated all their debts and credits. He kept insisting on going straight to the bottom line—custody of Meredith's daughter.

"All right, Mr. Logan," she reluctantly conceded, "you've made yourself perfectly—if rather crudely—clear. We'll play this thing your way."

"Big of you, Ms. Fletcher," Gabe responded, giving her an irreverent salute. "Okay, here it is, the bottom line. Mandy is my brother's child."

"And my sister's," Erica added quickly.

"*And,*" he continued doggedly, "if you'll forgive the melodramatics—as Gary lay on the deathbed your dearest sister prepared for him—he asked me to take care of his daughter."

"I'm sure my sister would have asked the same of me if she'd had the time to do so," Erica declared, wondering if Meredith had even thought of Amanda as she faced her own death.

Gabe looked at her owlishly. "Really, Ms. Fletcher? If you'll remember, your sister had already written Mandy off, deserting her to head for parts unknown. Oh, no. As I see it, the Fletchers lost any rights they had when dear Meredith skipped town. And, I'm sure you'll remember," he added, flashing that same infuriating smile once more, "possession is nine-tenths of the law."

"So you plan to raise Amanda because it's your *duty?* A promise you'd made to your dying brother? Surely your brother wouldn't want you to sacrifice your life that way? Especially now, when I'm willing to take Amanda off your hands."

His hand itched to wipe that smug, superior look from her gorgeous, patrician face. Where did she get off, talking to him about sacrifice? "You still don't get it, do you, lady? Mandy is my brother's child, all I have left of him. I love her, and I'm going to keep her. That's it, the whole enchilada, end of story."

"Amanda is all *I* have left of *my* sister, you know," Erica pointed out, measuring her words carefully.

"Yeah, I know," Gabe replied maddeningly. "But she's one hundred percent Logan in looks, something I go down on my knees in thanks for every night."

Erica's eyes narrowed as she fought to control her temper. He was baiting her—deliberately needling her. "The fact remains, Amanda is half Fletcher. Surely you cannot mean to deny the child her heritage?"

Gabe shrugged. "So set up a trust fund for her education. Anything else she gets from me."

"Why are you being so stubborn?" Erica all but screeched, leaping to her feet. "Do you honestly expect me to believe you're going to sit there and tell me that Amanda will be better off living with *you?*"

"Cross my heart and hope to die," Gabe replied, grinning up at her. "As a matter of fact, I'm willing to sit here and tell you that Mandy would be better off living in the streets than living with you. I knew Meredith. Considering her selfish example and your patronizing claims, I'd say there's not a court in the land that would knowingly hand you another life to ruin."

"Who said anything about court?" Erica asked swiftly, whirling to face Gabe. A feeling of deep dread invaded her heart. "I see no need, Mr. Logan, to drag this thing through the courts."

Gabe realized he had accidentally hit upon a sore spot, and he had every intention of picking at the wound. "What's the matter, Ms. Fletcher? The thought of those tacky little tabloids getting hold of the story of Meredith's abandoned love child getting you all a flutter? Ah, come on, what's a little publicity? The Fletchers can take it. Although I imagine you're more used to seeing your name on the society and financial pages."

"You bastard!"

"Flattery will get you nowhere," Gabe chided her, wagging a finger in her direction.

"How can you say you love Amanda and with the next breath threaten to make her into a public spectacle?" Erica demanded, feeling at last she had scored a point.

"Mandy's young, Ms. Fletcher. Any scandal will blow over long before she's old enough to suffer from it. And as to why I would be so miserable as to take the matter to court," he added, shrugging, "if that's what I have to do to keep her, I'll do it."

"Oh, you're so smug, aren't you?" Erica sneered, no longer caring that she wasn't in complete control of her emotions.

"I'm not smug. If I were being smug, I'd just say the devil made me do it."

"With me as the devil?" she asked, already knowing his answer.

Gabe grinned, shrugging his broad shoulders. "If the tail and horns fit . . ."

Erica had learned the fine points of negotiation in her years spent heading up F and W. She knew when to retreat and wait for another day. Walking purposefully toward the French doors, she looked back at the infuriating man and warned him, "You may have won the first battle, Mr. Logan. But you haven't won the war. I'll be back tomorrow at eleven to continue this discussion. Perhaps by then you'll have something more to offer than snide remarks and infantile jokes."

"And threats, Ms. Fletcher. Don't forget the threats. Shall I set you a place for luncheon, madame?" Gabe called after her. "I'm not yet sure what I'll be serving, but it will definitely be something that doesn't require the use of a knife. I may be infantile, but I'm not stupid!''

Gabe winced as the door slammed behind Erica Fletcher's departing form, the impact shaking the glass panes until he was sure one or more of them would shatter. He gritted his teeth in the sudden stillness. Damn her! The woman saw Mandy as just another Fletcher possession. And he wasn't giving an innocent child up to the cold clutches of that corporate family. He would protect Mandy if it was the last thing he did.

He walked over to the French doors, prudently locking them. Then he stood and watched until Erica had started her car and driven off before going down the hall, to quietly push open the door and enter Mandy's darkened bedroom.

The small Donald Duck night-light cast a glow on the pink walls and highlighted Mandy's perfect features. She had lost the pacifier once more, substituting her thumb for the ugly plastic "plug," and Gabe smiled as he watched a small frown form between her eyes as she sucked furiously.

One hand pressed to his mouth, Gabe dropped to his haunches beside the crib, staring intently at this child who had become his entire world, his reason for living.

He hadn't handled himself very well tonight. Erica Fletcher's identity had come as a major shock. After three months of silence, he had begun to believe no one would question his custody of Gary's daughter. Then he had compounded matters with his overdone sarcasm, his righteous anger, his undoubtedly transparent dislike for anyone bearing the name Fletcher.

She was gone now, but she'd be back. As surely as the sun would come up tomorrow, as surely as Mandy would wake with that sunrise, demanding her bottle, Gabe knew that Erica Fletcher would be back. Her kind didn't give up. If her sister had possessed half her backbone, a quarter of her intelligence and determination, Mandy would never have lost her parents.

"But she didn't, Mandy, baby," he whispered, slipping his hand through the bars of the crib to stroke the child's small cheek with the side of his ink-stained index finger, the difference in their sizes, astounding him as usual, reminding him of how helpless Mandy was, how she depended on him for everything. "*She* didn't care about anyone but herself, and now you have nobody but me to watch out for you. We're not going to count your Aunt Erica, because she won't be around for long. You're mine now, Mandy—my little sweetheart, my best girl. There isn't enough money in the world to change that. So don't you worry. Uncle Gabe is going to take care of that wicked F and W lady—one way or the other."

Erica seethed as she repeatedly pressed her manicured finger against Gabe's doorbell. "I told him I'd be here at eleven," she groused out loud as she looked down at her gold wristwatch, just to be sure she wasn't early. No, it was already almost five minutes past the hour. The man simply wasn't here—or he was hiding behind the drawn draperies, afraid to face her.

While one part of her rejoiced in Gabe's obvious admission of weakness—why would he hide if he had nothing to fear—another part of her wanted the meeting over and done with so that she could put this distasteful chapter of her life behind her as quickly as possible.

Reluctant to leave the premises, unwilling to admit defeat and place the matter in the hands of her lawyers, Erica strolled around the flagstone path leading to the rear of the house. Once she turned the corner, she could see Logan sprawled belly down on the grass, his head bobbing up and down as he seemed to be attacking something on the fluffy blanket spread out in front of him.

"Whose fat belly is this?" She could hear him asking in a silly, singsong voice. "I'm gonna get that fat belly, yes I am. Here I come, Mandy, *brrr!* Got ya!"

As Erica moved closer she could see the pudgy bare arms and legs that could belong only to her niece. Gabe's dark head was buried in the child's midsection. Again and again the man played the game with the happy child, her squeals and flailing limbs indicating her delight.

Unbidden, and totally unexpected, Erica felt a wave of loneliness swamp her, nearly bowling her over. Gabe may have lost his brother, but at least he had Amanda. She, Erica, had nothing—no one. Stock options were nice, but you couldn't hug them very well, and they never hugged you back.

Erica tiptoed closer and bent down to get her first really good look at Meredith's child. The baby had a thick thatch of dark hair—a perfect match to her uncle's, actually—and the pink and white complexion of a healthy infant. Clad only in a diaper, her chubby body seemed unbelievably perfect, as did her delicate facial features. A strange emotion slowly squeezed Erica's heart, and she had to blink rapidly to keep the sudden moistness in her eyes from spilling over onto her cheeks.

"You, er, you were wr-wrong," she stammered at last, barely recognizing her own voice. "She's got Meredith's sapphire-blue eyes."

Gabe rolled over so quickly that Mandy, who had been reveling in her uncle's attention, emitted a startled cry. "Now look what you've done!" Gabe growled, sweeping the child up into his arms to soothe her.

Erica felt an unfamiliar stab of envy at the sight of the baby snuggling so confidently into the man's bronzed shoulder. "I can see you've forgotten our appointment," she said, running her gaze insolently down his naked upper torso and past the faded cutoff jeans and crossed legs to his bare feet. "Or were you so caught up in your game that you simply lost track of the time?"

Gabe stared at her stonily. "Gary and I also have blue eyes. And I didn't lose track of the time. I just thought you had enough intelligence to give up. I didn't think you'd keep banging your head against a wall once you figured out how much it hurt."

"And what is that supposed to mean?" Erica prompted, trying hard not to watch Amanda's dimpled little fingers as they wove themselves through the dark curls on the man's chest.

"It means nothing's changed, a fact I thought you'd understand once you got your Fletcher ego back under control and realized Mandy's in good hands."

Erica looked at those hands, large, well-formed hands that lovingly cradled the child against his body, and found herself wondering if she, too, could feel so contented within their embrace. She shook her head, as if to get rid of such distracting thoughts. "Did you really think I'd fold my tent, as it were, and steal off into the night without even seeing Amanda?"

"As I recall, you didn't seem very interested in seeing her last night," Gabe countered. He rose gracefully to his full height, which placed the top of his head clearly a half foot higher than Erica's five feet six inches. "Here," he offered, surprising her by holding the baby out to her. "Say hello to each other while I go get us something cold to drink."

Extending her hands automatically, Erica somehow found her arms full of warm, wiggling infant, a child who suddenly seemed to have more limbs than an octopus. She had longed for this moment, but now that it had happened, she hadn't the foggiest idea what to do. "Wa-wait!" she exclaimed fearfully as Gabe began to lope off toward the back door of the house.

Turning to throw a knowing grin her way, he teased, "Don't worry, she doesn't bite—at least not yet."

"I'm not worried about myself, you idiot. What about Amanda? Her head—?" Erica questioned fearfully. "What do I do about her head?"

Gabe shrugged. "You could try kissing it, I guess. Jeez, and you want to raise her?"

"But I'd hire a nanny," Erica pointed out in a small voice as the screen door banged closed behind Gabe. Then Amanda's inquisitive fingers found a new home in her aunt's mouth, and any further arguments were curtailed while Erica struggled to shift the child.

After a few false starts Erica, still terrified, repositioned the baby so that she lay in the crook of her arm. But the child, probably sensing the anxiety of the person holding her, puckered up her little rosebud mouth and let out a fearful wail.

"Oh, my God," Erica whispered, devastated. "Don't cry, Amanda. Please don't cry. Here," she bargained in desperation, "I'll just lay you down on this blanket and we'll play until your nasty uncle comes back. Just, please, darling, don't let him hear you cry."

Handling the child with all the care she normally reserved for fifth-century Oriental vases, Erica deposited the infant on the blanket, thankful to have made the transfer from shaky arms to soft velour without mishap. Amanda stopped whimpering and Erica at last relaxed enough to take a good look at her niece.

Look at her, and fall instantly, deeply and completely in love.

"Look at you," she intoned softly, tears stinging her eyes as she gently captured one plump foot between her fingers. "You should be dressed in pretty white organdy, not left half naked like this. And I bet you'd be adorable in pink. Oh," she said laughing as Amanda tilted her head slightly, as if to listen to the unfamiliar female voice, "you'd like that, wouldn't you? We'll have to get you a whole new wardrobe once we get you home."

As she talked, Erica allowed her hands to trail over the baby's body, marveling at both its softness and its stunning, if miniature, perfection.

Look at her, Erica told herself. *Look at the way she's staring at me, almost as if she's sizing me up and deciding if I'm friend or foe.* Self-consciously checking to see if that infuriating Gabriel Logan was anywhere in sight, Erica tentatively lowered her head to Amanda's soft belly and, in imitation of Gabe's actions, blew soft bubbles against the infant's skin.

Would it work as well without the mustache? It did. Her hands and feet flailing, the baby emitted what Erica would have sworn was a giggle.

Pleased beyond anything in her memory—any boardroom fight hard won, any successfully closed business deal—Erica repeated the action again and again, while Amanda's pudgy fingers wreaked havoc on her aunt's carefully constructed hairdo.

That was how Gabe found them when he returned to the backyard, a tray with two glasses of lemonade and a bottle of formula in his hands. "Well, I'll be damned," he whispered as he watched the bright sunlight dancing in Erica's softly curling blond hair. "The woman looks almost human."

Oblivious to Gabe's presence, Erica was indulging herself in a way she hadn't in years. Discarding her carefully constructed veneer of sophistication, she was concentrating on the pure enjoyment of the moment. But all too soon Amanda tired of the game and began demanding her lunch.

"Oh, sweetheart, what's wrong?" Erica questioned uncertainly when Amanda's full lower lip began to tremble. The baby's face screwed itself up in preparation of letting go with a hearty demand to be fed. "Did Aunt Erica hurt you? Oh, please, darling, don't cry. If you cry he'll hear you and blame me."

"No, he won't," Gabe contradicted, dropping to his knees beside the blanket. "Here." He handed her the baby bottle. "It's feeding time at the zoo. Why don't you take care of Mandy while I go back inside and make us some sandwiches?"

Erica eyed the bottle as if it were about to attack her. "Feed her?" she asked in a thin, reedy voice. She might already love this child she hadn't seen until a few minutes ago, but she hadn't the faintest idea what to do with her!

Gabe could barely keep from laughing. "Yes, feed her. Or did you think babies were all goo-goo and tickle," he added as he rose to his feet and returned inside the house.

"I could learn to hate that man with very little effort," Erica told the world at large, determined to sit on the grass and do nothing until Gabe deigned to reappear. But Amanda had other ideas. Her wails became a full-fledged bout of bloodcurdling screams, with hiccuping sobs thrown in here and there for good measure. Defeated on all sides, Erica bowed to her fate.

Erica wasn't entirely stupid. She did have a basic idea of what was required of her now. Gingerly gripping Amanda behind the knees and neck, she carefully shifted the infant back into her arms and aimed the nipple toward Amanda's gaping mouth.

The resulting peace was miraculous. The hungry infant sucked greedily at the bottle, as if she had been hovering on the brink of starvation.

Of course, Amanda would eventually have to be burped. Erica was sure of this, even if she wasn't sure *why* babies indulged in such a disgusting habit. After Amanda had nursed for about ten minutes, Erica pried the nipple from the still avidly sucking mouth and carefully lifted the baby onto her shoulder.

Amanda howled, belligerent at having her lunch taken away. Erica patted, softly at first, and then more firmly as the feather-light taps didn't seem to be working. At last she was rewarded by a satisfying sound, only to discover that it had been a decidedly moist burp. Warm formula wended its way down the back of Erica's stylish dress and dribbled wetly over her shoulder to slide down her bare arm.

"Oh, Amanda," Erica groaned. "How could you?"

But Amanda wasn't in an explaining moód. She was once again ravenous, and it was all Erica could do to direct the nipple back toward the seeking mouth. "Greedy, little monster, aren't you?" her aunt chided, mentally consigning her dress to the rag bag. "As your uncle said, you certainly do resemble the Logans. We'll have to do something about those table manners of yours, that's for sure."

Gabe, who had been watching from the kitchen window, hoping with all his heart that Mandy would perform just as she had, was oddly disappointed at Erica's nonchalant reaction. He had thought she'd be screaming by now, demanding that he take the "little brat" away.

He had to hand it to the woman, she had even more backbone than he had given her credit for last night. Acting against his better judgment, he decided to rescue her before Mandy performed her one remaining party trick.

An hour later Amanda had been changed and settled into her crib for a nap. Her aunt and uncle had eaten their own lunch on the sun-drenched patio. Now the time had come for some serious discussion of the infant's future.

"You didn't think I could do it, did you?" Erica asked, smugly picking up the empty baby bottle as she watched Gabe drain the last of the lemonade from his glass.

"Who, me?" he asked with mock innocence. "What do you mean?"

"Don't try to get out of it," Erica warned, warming to this outrageous man in spite of herself. "You deliberately threw Amanda at my head, hoping I'd run out of here screaming, never to be heard from again."

Gabe avoided her eyes. "I'll admit the thought may have crossed my mind."

Erica shook her head, then pushed an errant lock of light blond hair behind her ear. "You know it doesn't matter, anyway. I've already made inquiries with an agency in Philadelphia concerning a nurse for Amanda. Would you believe they still call them nannies?"

All the good feelings that had been building up inside Gabe for this beautiful creature drained away rapidly as the full meaning of her words hit home. "So," he said, a decided chill descending on the patio as he spoke, "you plan to hand Mandy over to strangers. How very upper-crust of you. Tell me, did you and Meredith have nannies?"

"Of course we did. Until we were ten and went away to boarding school in Vermont. What else did you expect?"

" 'Of course we did,' " Gabe parroted in a parody of her precise, finishing-school accent. "And using you and your sister as examples of this method of child rearing, you expect me to hand Mandy over so that she can grow up just like you two? Spare me, lady, spare me."

"Well, what else do you suggest I do? I can't give her up. Not now!" Erica shot back angrily. Talk about going back to square one! They had regressed way beyond that point, thanks to his stubbornness.

All that could be heard for some minutes were birds chirping in the surrounding oak trees, as Gabe sat deep in thought, mulling a crazy idea over in his head. It had to be a crazy idea; it was too illogical, too wildly improbable, to be anything else. He had thought of it late last night, sitting alone in the den, and he quickly dismissed it. But it might work. It just might work. What did he have to lose? He might as well give it a try. That business about a nanny had settled it for him.

"Well?" Erica prodded at last. "How long do I have to wait for you to come down from that mountaintop with your words of wisdom?"

At long last, a cunning look stealing onto his handsome face, Gabe spoke. "Come live with us," he suggested baldly, spreading his arms wide in a gesture of welcome.

"That's it? That's your solution? 'Come live with us.' *Are you crazy?*" Erica gripped the edge of the metal picnic table with both hands as she leaned across its surface, her green eyes spitting fire.

Rising so swiftly that her chair toppled over onto the concrete, she threw up her arms and swung about in a full circle before pressing her palms on the tabletop and glaring at him. "You're not playing with a full deck, Mr. Logan, do you know that? Good God. My niece is living with a lunatic."

"Oh, sit down," Gabe told her, ignoring her outburst, even if he couldn't totally ignore how beautiful she looked in a temper. "If you'll only think about it a moment you'll see it's the perfect solution."

"Really?" Erica's voice dripped with sarcasm. Reluctantly she straightened her chair and sat down. "Tell me, do artists always make five of two and two, or are you the exception?"

"Don't push, lady," Gabe warned, beginning to feel he had just made one doozy of a mistake.

"Heavens, no, I shouldn't push," Erica agreed, shaking her head. "One never knows when your sort could turn violent. You know, the sooner I get Amanda away from you, the happier I'll be—"

"My point exactly," Gabe cut in, effectively putting an end to Erica's tirade. He had started this, and he was going to finish it!

Deliberately making a major project out of piling up the lunch plates, Gabe outlined his plan. She would move in, on a trial basis, so that she could learn how to care for the child. Once he was convinced that she could handle Mandy, and once she promised to take a more active part in Mandy's everyday care, he would allow her custody—providing he retained extensive visiting rights and a vote in any major decisions affecting his niece's life.

"But I've got the family business to consider," Erica pointed out in what she hoped was a rational way. "I don't just play at F and W, you know. I'm CEO, for crying out loud. I have heavy responsibilities. I'd never be able to be a full-time mother to Amanda, so what's the point in learning how to change diapers?"

Gabe shook his head reprovingly. "I always heard that a good boss should never ask anything of an employee that he—or she—can't do. How will you know if Mandy's care is adequate? A child needs stability in its life, you can't just keep discarding nannies until you get a good one."

Erica gnawed on her bottom lip, trying hard to find a way to punch holes in Gabe's theory. But he was right, damn him. "All right. But why can't you and

Amanda come to Philadelphia? Why does it all have
to be your way?''

The smile Erica was learning to hate was back.
''Because, as the saying goes, it's *my* football. We play
my way or we don't play at all.''

''I shouldn't have bothered to ask. How long would
I have to live here?'' she asked, narrowing her eyes as
she tried to envision the two of them inhabiting the
ranch house without killing each other.

Gabe shrugged. She was buying it; she was really
buying it! ''Until I'm satisfied that you won't feed
Mandy quiche for lunch—or wash her down the drain
when you give her a bath.''

''But that could be months—'' Erica bit off her
words before she could dig her grave any deeper, seeing the gleam in Gabe's eyes. ''I mean, how long could
it take to learn a few basic child-care skills? A week?
Two?''

''Let's compromise and say three weeks.''

''Three weeks? But I can't be away from F and W
that long.''

''Okay.'' Gabe nodded, rising to his feet and gathering up the plates to take them into the kitchen. ''So
much for your love for Mandy. Give us a call next time
you're in town, why don't you? I'll tell Mandy you
said goodbye.'' He turned and began walking toward
the house, mentally counting to ten. He only got to
five before she called after him.

''Wait a minute! Let's talk about this some more.''

Gabe turned his head and looked at her quizzically,
determined not to give her an inch. They'd do this his
way or they wouldn't do it at all. Besides, even if she
accepted his offer, she'd be out of here within the
week, running as fast as she could back to her cushy

mainline mansion. So why did he suddenly feel so sorry for her?

"Lady," he said, turning around, his words more honest than either of them could believe, "you want to know something? You're beginning to get on my nerves."

Chapter Three

So many thoughts were racing around in Erica's brain that she was beginning to feel slightly dizzy. What an insufferable man! One moment he was opening his house to her, being generous almost to a fault, and the next minute he was dismissing her like some unwanted door-to-door salesman. Was it his artistic temperament, or was he deliberately trying to drive her crazy?

"You have to give me a few minutes to think about this," she said quickly, as he once again headed toward the back door.

He kept on walking, halting only momentarily as Erica raced ahead and opened the screen door for him. "What do you need to think about? You left your precious business for nearly a year to go gallivanting around the globe, didn't you? What's a few weeks?" he asked.

"I had planned for that trip, and I was in daily contact with my people here." As Erica spoke she looked about the large kitchen, and was not very impressed by what she saw.

"So? The telephone works between Allentown and Philly," Gabe pointed out. "Come on. There must be more. Spit it out."

The kitchen was brown. *Brown,* for heaven's sake! Cabinets, appliances, even the tile floor. Whoever heard of a totally brown kitchen? There were no curtains, no flowers, not a single hint of its user being the least bit interested in anything but using the room for its admitted purpose—feeding his face!

"Would I really have to *live* here?" she groaned, her pained expression clearly showing her distaste.

"Mandy still takes bottles at ten at night and six in the morning—sometimes five-thirty. You'd never manage it any other way." Depositing the beige plastic dishes into the already full sink, Gabe haphazardly ran some water over them and then turned his back on the entire mess. "Any other questions?"

"May I have meals sent in?" Erica asked hesitantly, more afraid of food poisoning than inciting her host's wrath. "I mean, it's just that I don't cook very well, just sandwiches and that sort of thing, and...and it looks like you could use a vacation from kitchen duty. I'd order enough for two."

Nodding his head in wry acknowledgement, Gabe pushed himself away from the sink and led the way into the living room.

It was also brown. A brown couch sat on the brown wall-to-wall carpeting. Twin brown leather armchairs with matching ottomans stood in front of the brown and beige striped draperies. Fall landscapes, mostly brown with touches of orange, hung on beige walls. Erica took three steps into the room, stopped dead and put her hands on her hips. "I can't believe it! This place has all the charm of a bus station. And you're an artist?"

Gabe looked around the room as if he were seeing it for the first time. "This was Gary's house. Since he was the youngest, Mom and Dad left it to him in their will. I only moved in after Gary's death, figuring it was easier than trying to raise Mandy in a high-rise apartment."

"I—I'm sorry," Erica stammered. "I didn't mean to imply your family had bad taste."

His blue eyes twinkling, Gabe was clearly amused at her discomfiture at calling his family names while she had been more than eager to insult *him*. "Oh, that's all right. You may have a small point about Gary's lack of taste. After all, he did choose your sister."

Immediately the animosity between them was back in full force. Raising her finely sculpted chin, Erica asked to be shown the room she would be using—*if* she agreed to his crazy proposal.

Just off the hallway, to the left of the small foyer, was the bedroom. Filled with Queen Anne furniture, it was a pleasant surprise. A white hobnail bedspread, an inexpensive but tasteful Oriental rug, and white organdy priscilla curtains all served to indicate that this was one room Gary's redecorating had not destroyed.

"It's lovely," Erica exclaimed with more relief than admiration in her voice.

Leaning against the doorjamb, Gabe took in the sight of Erica standing in the middle of the room, the midday sun casting a golden halo around her body. "Yes," he agreed thoughtfully. "Lovely."

Something in Gabe's voice warned her that they were talking about two different things, and Erica quickly busied herself inspecting the large closet and private bath attached to the room. As every bedroom in the large Fletcher home had its own bathroom, it did not occur to her that Gabe had allotted her the best bedroom in the house.

"Mandy's in the room next to yours, and I'm on the other side of the hall. If you want the rest of the nickel tour, I'll show you my office. It's in the same wing as the family room and laundry."

"Office?" Erica questioned, ducking under Gabe's arm. She looked longingly toward the closed door to Amanda's room, wishing the child would wake. She didn't like being alone with the baby's uncle. "Don't you mean your studio?"

Following Erica down the hallway, Gabe tried to explain his description of his workplace as he reprimanded himself for some of the thoughts he had been entertaining since she had entered the bedroom. If Mandy wasn't sleeping just a few feet away...

"I'm a working man, Ms. Fletcher. I draw finely detailed pen-and-ink drawings to illustrate biology and medical textbooks. All I need is a desk and good light. I don't even need inspiration. My employers tell me what to draw, and I've always found hunger a great motivator. I'm drawing muscle tissue this week. Leg muscle."

"Oh," Erica breathed, disappointed. "I had it wrong, then, didn't I? I thought you were a real artist, not a technician." Somehow that took a lot of the excitement out of seeing his work. "I—I'll have to look at it some other time," she said, stopping so quickly that Gabe nearly ran into her. "I have to get back to check out of my motel. I want to get home before dark."

Gabe's stomach did an unexpected somersault. "Then you're not going to take me up on my offer?" he asked, hoping he didn't sound as disappointed as he suddenly felt at the thought of Erica Fletcher walking out of his life. He felt disgusted with himself. Of course he wanted her out of his life, out of Mandy's life. And he'd better not let himself forget that fact.

"On the contrary, Mr. Logan," she assured him, heading for the back door. "But I need to go back to Philadelphia to pack some clothes and take care of some business matters. And see my lawyer."

Erica had her hand on the screen door before Gabe could stop her. "Lawyer?" he repeated, looking down at her suspiciously.

"Of course," she supplied matter-of-factly. "I can't rely on a verbal agreement when it comes to something as important as my niece's future. I'll get my lawyer to draw up a contract based on your conditions. Naturally, I intend to add a few of my own, just to protect myself."

"Naturally," Gabe gritted out between clenched teeth. Her lovely blond hair might be hanging down around her shoulders, no longer scraped back from her face in that no-nonsense matter, but she was still every inch the businesswoman. "You're something else, lady, do you know that?" He shook his head in disgust, then lightly touched his index finger to the center of her chest. "What makes you tick, Ms. Fletcher? Surely there can't be a heart in there."

Caught off guard, Erica took a small involuntary step backward before her years of negotiating came to her rescue. "There's no need to descend to insults, Mr. Logan. Can't you understand that I'm entitled to some protection?"

Gabe ran his gaze up and down her body and then let out a dismissing laugh. "You? I think you're quite capable of protecting yourself."

Erica ignored this jibe just as she was sure she would have to overlook much of what Gabriel Logan would say in the weeks to come. "My conditions are simple. One, my duties in this house will involve only Amanda, and two, you keep your distance."

Gabe could feel his hands bunching into fists. "It's a damn shame your sister wasn't so careful. If she had put her affair with Gary into writing, maybe he would have been smart enough to run away before he got in over his head."

"Oh, yes, thank you for reminding me," Erica went on, happy to be back on a formal footing with the strangely disturbing man who stood in front of her, nearly naked in his cutoff jeans. "There is a further condition. There will be no more sniping about Meredith. She was Amanda's mother, just as your brother was her father. If anything, you can restrain your snide comments out of respect for Amanda."

After a moment, Gabe nodded. "All right. No more cracks about Meredith."

"And the other conditions? It's ridiculous to have my lawyer draw up the contract if you're going to refuse to sign it."

Crossing his arms over his bare chest, Gabe appeared to give her words his deep consideration. His movement made his muscles ripple, and brought a faint, unexpected flush to Erica's cheeks.

"All right," he said at last, holding out his right hand. "Your duties will be limited to caring for Mandy." As Erica put her pale hand in his tan one, he added thoughtfully, "But I have to see for myself whether or not the second condition is necessary."

Before Erica could draw away, Gabe pulled her none too gently against his chest and lifted her chin so that his mouth could capture hers.

He had meant to startle her, shake her out of her professional-businesswoman-satisfactorily-concluding-a-deal posture. But he had not counted on the softness of her lips, the dangerous way her body fitted against his, or the tremor of desire that started low in his body and quickly spread.

When Erica's hands moved up to his shoulders to push him away, she, in turn, was unprepared for the tingling sensation she felt as her fingertips encountered his smooth, warm flesh. Instead of curling into fists to beat him away, her hands betrayed her as her fingers spread themselves wide and indulged in a fevered exploration of his hard upper body.

Suddenly she was being pushed away, nearly falling. Erica fought the urge to rub her upper lip where his mustache had brushed against it. She would have ripped off a blistering comment, if only she could force anything vaguely resembling coherent speech past her constricted throat. As it was, she had to content herself with giving Gabe a look that should have curled his bare toes.

Gathering her shattered composure about her like a cloak, Erica passed a trembling hand through her badly mussed hair. Then she motioned for Gabe to stand aside and let her pass.

Gabe nonchalantly shoved the screen door open and bowed her out onto the patio. "Did I scare you off, ice lady?" he asked insolently as she brushed past, doing his best to pretend that holding her, kissing her, hadn't affected him.

"I'll be back Saturday morning, Mr. Logan," Erica tossed over her shoulder as her heels clicked sharply against the flagstone path. "*With* the contract *and* all three conditions!"

"Don't flatter yourself, lady," Gabe, leaning around the edge of the screen door, called after her. "I've had better kisses from my Great-aunt Gertrude!"

Erica stopped dead in her tracks, her entire body stiffening as she considered whether or not it was worth her time to go back and argue. Weighing Amanda's future against momentary satisfaction, she decided against it. The day she and her niece left this house forever would be satisfaction enough. "The ground rules still stand," she bit out, then headed for her car.

As Gabe leaned against the screen door, watching Erica's silk-encased derriere move away from him, he commented under his breath, "And haven't you heard, Ms. Fletcher, that rules were made to be broken?"

He hadn't thought she would really take him up on his offer. He'd made it partly as a joke, and partly because of some half-baked notion that it would scare her off for good. Gabe had been caught off guard by her quick acceptance of his terms.

But as he had shown her around Gary's house, the full impact of his suggestion had hit him. Erica Fletcher was a determined woman. What if she really did manage to stick it out? What if she became genuinely concerned for the child? Had he actually opened his big mouth and spoken the words that could cost him Mandy—the only person he loved?

"Not if I have anything to say about it!" he muttered into the silence of the family room, having put Mandy down for the night some minutes earlier. And then, unbelievably, he laughed at himself. Hadn't he *said* enough already?

Taking a deep, satisfying drink from the cold bottle of beer he usually enjoyed at the end of a long day, Gabe reminded himself once again that he did not like Erica Fletcher. He didn't like her, what she stood for, her resemblance to Meredith, or the memories she provoked. The last thing he wanted, the very last thing, was for Erica, or any Fletcher, to have anything to do with Mandy.

He should have left well enough alone. His threat of a court suit certainly had rattled her cage. Why couldn't he have been satisfied with that?

"Because she wasn't about to go away," he reminded himself aloud. She was going to stick around like a bad summer cold until he either strangled her or threw her to the floor and made mad, passionate love with her. He looked at the half-empty bottle of beer in disgust and slammed it down on the end table.

"This plan of yours had better work, Logan," he told himself severely.

Maybe Mandy would begin to cut all her baby teeth in the next three weeks. That would send her aunt screaming from the premises, vowing never to return.

It was either that, or he would have to launch a major seduction of the lady to scare her away.

Gabe picked up the beer and finished it in one unsatisfying gulp, and then sat absentmindedly folding the pile of diapers that sat on the coffee table, still trying to understand what was really bothering him.

An hour later, he figured it out.

Crazily, he felt angry that she didn't like him. And Erica Fletcher had made one thing crystal clear: she didn't like him one little bit.

Erica spent the evening in the plush Fletcher drawing room, curled up on the white satin Sheraton sofa looking through old photograph albums. Meredith was featured in more of the photographs than she, mostly due to the fact that her younger sister had always been delighted to pose for the camera while Erica, hiding either thin, knobby knees, braces on her teeth, or, in her later teens, her dreadfully late blooming figure, had always tried to make herself scarce every time a camera was in sight.

Meredith had been such a beautiful child, all golden curls and pink cheeks. Amanda, bless her, was also beautiful, but Erica had to agree with Logan's assessment. Aside from the color of her eyes, the baby bore no resemblance to her mother. "I think she may have my chin," she mused aloud, looking at a photograph of herself as an infant. "Oh, dear, I hope her teeth will come in straight."

Erica had reached the sprawling suburban Fletcher estate just in time for Mrs. James to prepare a simple if generous dinner, clucking her tongue as she always did as she complained about Miss Erica eating no more than would keep a bird alive. After toying with her meal, Erica called Bob Abernathy, the family lawyer, and made an appointment to meet with him early the next morning.

She had made a cursory attempt to sort through her wardrobe in preparation for packing, but when she realized she was weighing each outfit as to whether or not it would appeal to Gabriel Logan, she threw down an armful of dresses in disgust. She would pack tomorrow, after a good night's sleep.

Try as she might, she could not bring herself to go into Meredith's room. When Mrs. James came into the living room to say good-night, Erica asked her if she would be willing to sort out her sister's things and arrange for everything to be given to a local charity.

"And about time, too," Mrs. James muttered as she nodded her head vigorously. "A body could clothe half a country with that one's duds."

Erica flinched at the words. Learning that her longtime housekeeper had little love for her departed sister was too much reality for her to face in one day. Some illusions had to die slowly, if any of the good memories were to survive.

Later that night, after spending more than an hour tossing and turning, Erica slipped out of bed and crept to her window. Looking out over the moonlit gardens, she wondered why, after the exhausting day and long drive, she still had trouble falling asleep.

Thoughts of Amanda—the feel of her soft, warm body snuggled close in her arms—kept intruding on her peace, filling her with anxiety. She had to have that child! Nothing could happen to ruin her chance of wresting Amanda away from that dreadful man and that dreary house. She would do anything, even live under his roof, to gain her objective.

A showdown in court must be avoided at all costs. Although she found it hard to believe anyone who loved a child could subject it to such harmful publicity, she realized that Gabriel Logan was as desperate as she. If she dared to cross him, he might just make good on his threat.

Maybe that was why she couldn't sleep. Gabe's offer was so contrary to his earlier stubbornness. Why had he suggested this absurd plan? What did he hope to gain? What was his angle? Did he really think a few messy diapers would be enough to change her mind about wanting Amanda?

It didn't make sense. Holding the upper hand, as it were, why had he agreed to compromise? Perhaps, she thought suddenly, he was tired of playing the doting uncle. She quickly dismissed that thought. If Gabe had wanted his freedom he would have accepted her offer to take Amanda off his hands—and even profited on the deal.

She lowered her forehead against the windowpane, her thoughts beginning to give her a headache. Why was she beating herself by looking for logical reasons behind anything Gabriel Logan might do? The man wasn't worth it. No matter what outlandish demands he made, she would agree to them—as long as he was willing to sign on the dotted line of the contract Bob would be drawing up in the morning. And within a month she would be able to forget the man ever existed.

She crept back into bed and willed her body to relax, refusing to think about how she hoped Bob would be able to find a way around the visitation section of the contract.

After all, as the man had said, possession was nine-tenths of the law.

Erica sat in a quiet corner of the Allentown library, her attention fully focused on the microfiche reproduction of the local newspaper. The picture above the story showed a mass of twisted, blackened metal that must have once been a car. It hurt her just to look at it.

Local Celebrity Injured in Fiery One Car Crash; Drunken Driving Probable Cause. She read the bold black headline twice, her lips silently mouthing the words, before leaning back against the uncomfortable wooden chair, her eyes closed in pain. She hadn't been the only one who'd had to deal with a sensational press. On a smaller scale, Gabriel Logan had had to deal with it, too.

Cursing herself for being needlessly nosy, yet determined to find out as much about Gary Logan as possible, she sat forward once more and read the article.

Gary Logan, 26, of Beaver Valley Road, Allentown, Route One, was severely injured early this morning in a fiery one car crash in Salisbury Township. Preliminary police reports indicate Logan was intoxicated at the time of the crash that totaled the sports car and caused a fire that destroyed a vacant barn.

Logan, owner of the Logan Ice Skating School, and one time Olympic Bronze Medalist, has been transferred by helicopter to a Philadelphia burn center where his condition is listed as critical.

Erica didn't bother reading any more of the article. Instead, she searched through the microfiche for Gary

Logan's obituary, hoping that his "celebrity" status would have merited that his photograph be run with the story.

It did. Erica bit her bottom lip as she stared at the handsome young man with the open, trusting face. He looked a lot like his brother, except that he was finer boned and clean shaven. The picture also showed her that Gary Logan's personality had been vastly different from Gabe's.

This was a man who had trusted, a man who had loved life. A man, Erica knew, who would have taken one look at her beautiful, helpless sister and lost his heart. They must have been like children, playing at romance until the reality of a newborn baby had sent Meredith running for her freedom.

Erica scanned the obituary notice, noting that, as Gabe had told her, he was his brother's sole surviving relative other than "a daughter, Amanda."

"What a waste," Erica concluded quietly, turning off the microfiche reader. "What a terrible, senseless waste."

"If you're finished here, miss, I'll take care of putting everything away."

Erica looked up blankly at the library clerk. "Thank you," she said, rising, "that's very kind of you." She looked at her watch, noting that it was nearly five o'clock, closing time. "You've been most helpful."

She walked out into the bright sunlight and headed for her car. She'd been in Allentown since early that afternoon, shopping, sight-seeing, doing anything she could do to put off the moment she would have to ring Gabriel Logan's doorbell, suitcase in hand, and relinquish control of her life—if only for the next three weeks.

But now she had run out of things to do, places to go. It was time to head out to the house on Beaver Valley Road.

The drive along Hamilton Boulevard was lovely, with grassy hills and a small lake bordering it on one side for more than a mile. Large, handsome houses and a few discreet businesses dotted the other edge of the roadway.

Once farther out of the city, past the large Dorney Amusement Park, she put on her directional signal and turned onto the narrow macadam road that curved down toward a small, wooden glen. Turning left two blocks farther on, she realized that although she would still be close to the city, Gabe's house was fairly isolated, with the closest neighbor more than a block away.

The thought of living in that house with Gabe, day in, day out, with only a three-month-old child to act as chaperon, sent a knot of fear into Erica's suddenly tight chest. "Don't be ridiculous," she had told Bob Abernathy that morning when the lawyer had warned her that she could be opening herself up to more trouble than she needed. "The man wouldn't be so stupid as to do anything to jeopardize his only chance for a sizable settlement once he agrees to my custody of Amanda."

Now, only a few hours after her brave denial, Erica was having second thoughts. Pulling the car onto the gravel driveway and cutting the engine, she corrected herself. She wasn't having second thoughts. She was having third thoughts. And fourth, and fifth.

"This is crazy—completely crazy!" she declared, restarting the engine in the hope of backing out of the drive and speeding back to Philadelphia as fast as she could. "Bob should have had me committed the moment I told him what I was planning to do."

Turning to make sure there was nothing behind her, Erica put the car into reverse and her foot on the gas—just as another car pulled into the driveway behind her.

What terrible timing! It was Gabriel Logan.

She slammed her foot onto the brake, then sat facing forward, staring at nothing while behind her she heard the sound of a car door slamming closed, then, a few moments later, another slam. A frown creased her forehead. Two car doors? Who was with him? She shot a quick look in her rearview mirror and saw Gabe walking toward her, Amanda in his arms. Erica sighed, not realizing it was with relief. Amanda must have been in a baby carrier in the back seat.

"Hi there." Gabe's voice was close—too close—to her ear. "You've got great timing, Ms. Fletcher. Mandy and I just went out to get our dinner."

"Dinner?" Erica repeated, stealing a look at him. He was standing beside her door, dressed in casual tan slacks and a black pullover shirt, his arms full of her sleeping niece, a large brown bag and a carton of soda. "What do you have in there?"

"Super-hoagies and French fries," he answered, hefting the bag, which she could see was stained with grease. "It's the Saturday night special down at Marge's. You'll love it. Unless you have something against salami?"

Erica closed her eyes and shook her head. "I must be out of my mind," she muttered fatalistically, opening the door and holding out her hands for her niece. As Amanda's warm, sleeping body curled trustingly against her, the spark of maternal instinct she had hoped for on their first meeting at last flared into life. She felt completely at home with the baby on her shoulder, as if she had been born to hold this child, love this child.

Smiling, and at last feeling as if everything was going to be all right, Erica turned for the house, leaving Gabe to follow in her wake. "Of course I like salami," she said breezily. "Do you have any antacid in the house, Mr. Logan?"

Gabe checked on Mandy one last time before going to the kitchen. He stood in front of the open refrigerator for five full minutes before he realized that there was nothing in the house to eat—or at least nothing that appealed to him anyway. Pulling a cold bottle of beer from the shelf on the refrigerator door, he twisted off the cap, tossed it in the general direction of the trash can, and made his way to the family room. He turned on the television set, not caring what was on, then flopped down onto his back on the soft leather couch.

What a day! The first half of it had flown by, right up until lunchtime, and the realization that Erica Fletcher wasn't going to show up to eat the meal he had nearly broken his neck preparing for them—*literally* almost broken his neck preparing for them. He had found his mother's recipe for tuna melt sandwiches somewhere and put them in the oven, then left the room to turn the buzzer off on the clothes dryer before the noise woke Mandy. When he had smelled the sandwiches burning under the broiler, he had raced into the kitchen, only to trip over one of Mandy's bibs and crash against the cabinets.

The tuna melt sandwiches had been consigned to the garbage, along with the remainder of Gabe's good intentions concerning a personally prepared welcome for Mandy's mainline aunt. Tuna melt sandwiches! What could he have been thinking? She'd probably never seen one before in her life.

The afternoon hadn't gone any better, with Mandy deciding to skip her nap, so that Gabe couldn't have cleaned up the house even if he'd wanted to, which he didn't—although he did run the vacuum over the living-room rug while cradling Mandy in his free arm. And he did do the dishes—all three days' worth, while Mandy reclined in her baby chair on the floor, cooing and inspecting her toes.

But did Erica Fletcher notice all his hard work? No, she did not. Did she appreciate how difficult it was to balance the responsibilities of a house and a baby and a job and still make them all work? No, she did not. Did she even bother to thank him for strapping Mandy in her car seat and driving all the way down to Marge's for super-hoagies and French fries? No, she most definitely did not.

Well, he thought meanly, taking a long pull on the beer bottle—and not for one moment thinking that he might be behaving like an overworked housewife angry with her ungrateful husband—*it will be a cold day in hell before I do anything nice for her again!*

And now Erica was down the hall—just down that one short hallway—sleeping in his parents' bed, probably with visions of dollar signs and mergers dancing in her head. Sleeping in his mother's bed— probably wearing something sheer and fluffy and low cut. Sleeping soundly, because he had told her he would handle Mandy if she woke during the night. Sleeping soundly because she was so blinking cocksure of herself, so ready to prove her ability to take care of Mandy, handle that damned "family business" long distance, put him firmly in his place—and probably eat fire and juggle knives at the same time!

She had only been in the house for a few hours and he no longer felt that he was in control. From her matched designer luggage—that he had somehow volunteered to lug into the bedroom—to the too neat pile of week-old newspapers she had stacked on the ottoman, to the soaking baby bottles lined up neatly next to the kitchen sink, to the scent of her faintly exotic perfume that lingered in the air, Erica Fletcher had already put her stamp all over *his* house.

"You've had some dumb plans in your lifetime, bucko," he told himself as he rose from the couch and deliberately knocked the too neat stack of newspapers onto the carpet as he headed for his bedroom, "but this one takes the prize! Sure, you still might be able to get her out of your house, but how are you going to get her out of your head? Huh? Tell me that one, bucko!"

Chapter Four

It was six-thirty in the morning and the sun was barely above the horizon. Erica had been abruptly awakened a half hour earlier by the sound of Mandy's crying—and the annoying slamming and banging of various assorted drawers and doors as Gabe crashed through the house, obviously wearing combat boots.

Erica wanted a cup of coffee.

No, it went deeper than that. She *needed* a cup of coffee. Terribly. Desperately. Enough to die for it. Enough to *kill* for it!

"Where in the name of heaven could that insane man possibly have hidden it?" she appealed aloud, running a hand through her unbound hair as she inspected the contents of yet another kitchen cabinet. She had spent a miserable, sleepless night, tossing and turning and wondering how in the world she had ever allowed herself to be talked into such an impossible scheme. She didn't need this; she didn't need it one single bit!

Yes, being with Amanda was wonderful, glorious, even if Gabe hadn't allowed her to do much more than hold the infant until it was time for her last bottle of the day. He still didn't trust her not to *break* the child or something, that much was certain, and Erica resented being kept away from her niece.

Determined not to spend any more time with Gabe than their agreement called for, she had gone to bed soon after Mandy had been put down for the night. But it had taken her a long time to fall asleep. Gabe had stayed behind in the family room, and the sounds coming from the large-screen television could not be blocked out by her bedroom door. Professional wrestling! She still couldn't believe the man had actually sat up until midnight watching professional wrestling.

He was even worse than she had supposed and definitely a bad influence on her niece. Once she had Amanda safely back in Philadelphia, Erica would find a way to deny him anything but the most stringent visitation rights. Mandy was a Fletcher, and Fletchers shouldn't be exposed to professional wrestling.

Her teeth clenched as she put her hands on her hips and shot a narrowed glance around the cluttered kitchen. Early morning sunlight poured in through the uncurtained window, hurting her eyes. "He's done this on purpose. I know he has. Damn the man. A person couldn't find a dead horse in this mess."

"My, my. May we take it, then, that we aren't a morning person? You're going to be great company for Mandy at six o'clock tomorrow morning. Poor baby, I hope she has it in her heart to forgive me. She's napping now, by the way. Bathed, too. But don't thank me. Sometimes I'm so efficient I amaze myself."

Erica whirled about in her silk wraparound dressing gown, the mint-green material swirling around her ankles. "You!" she accused hotly, hating the casual way he was lounging against the doorjamb.

"You got that in one. It's me all right," he agreed easily as he spread his arms and allowed her to complete her visual inventory. His bare legs were crossed at the ankles, and his long, lean body was once again covered only by a pair of faded cutoff jeans. An empty baby bottle dangled from his right hand, and a cloth diaper was draped over his left shoulder. He looked like a Greek god, and she hated him for it.

"What did you do with it?"

Gabe pushed himself away from the doorjamb and walked into the kitchen, eyeing the open cabinet doors both above and below the countertop. "What did I do with what? Are you on a search and destroy mission in my kitchen, Ms. Fletcher?" he asked, his face entirely too innocent for her liking. "Or are you planning to cook breakfast for us? And you said you didn't want to play house. Naughty, naughty, Ms. Fletcher."

Erica longed to bash him over the head with something—like the large frying pan that had fallen out of one of the cabinets a few minutes earlier and landed squarely on her big toe.

She spoke slowly, drawing out the question. "Where...do you...hide...the *coffee?* It took me five minutes to find a clean cup, there's no nondairy creamer anywhere, and you have only brown sugar in the house—and I found *that* in the refrigerator. You have got to be the most disorganized person in the world. Stop smiling at me like some mindless ape! Where the hell's the coffee?''

Gabe leaned back against the sink and folded his arms across his chest. "I'm not going to tell you. You haven't said the magic word," he pointed out, grinning at her so that she had a clear view of his whiter-than-white teeth in his tanned face.

If she were home in Philadelphia she'd be sitting on the terrace at a perfectly laid table complete with linen cloth, Limoges china, Waterford crystal and a small but perfect fresh flower centerpiece. As she leisurely read through the morning paper, Mrs. James would be hovering close by, ready to serve her. *With hot, fresh perked coffee!* She could smell its heady aroma wafting gently to her nostrils. She could almost taste its richness, savor its soothing effect on her jangled nerves.

Erica twined her fingers together in front of her and squeezed, hard, until her knuckles turned white. She wanted to tie him to an anthill and spread his stupid, hairy chest with orange marmalade. She wanted to dump him in a big black pot and boil him in oil. She wanted to urge him along with the tip of her saber as he walked the plank over a tank stocked with alligators. Hungry alligators. With great big pointy teeth.

"*Please* tell me where you hide the coffee," she growled, wishing looks could kill.

"Now, that wasn't so bad, was it? It probably didn't even hurt," Gabe said soothingly as he pushed himself away from the sink and opened the corner cabinet. "Here you go—coffee. I don't know how you missed it."

Erica stared at the jar in his hand, aghast. "That's instant coffee," she told him blankly. "I don't drink instant coffee. You have a coffeemaker on the counter over there. Where's the *real* coffee?''

Gabe cleared a spot where the L-shaped counters met and then hiked himself up onto it, his bare feet dangling a few inches from the floor. "The coffeemaker's broken. I think I was supposed to pour vinegar or something through it once in a while, but I always forgot. Instant's just as good. Trust me.''

"Instant coffee. No nondairy creamer. *Brown* sugar—probably to match the decor. Oh, no. Not me. Not in this lifetime anyway!" Erica turned on her heel and headed for the doorway.

"Now where are we going?" Gabe called after her, hopping down from his perch. "Wait for me. Don't tell me you're throwing in the towel already. You haven't even started taking care of Mandy yet."

Erica stopped in her tracks and turned around, just in time to come nose-to-nose with Gabe's bare chest. She had known he was tall, but now that she was barefoot she realized that he must be at least four inches over six feet. His bare shoulders were as broad as a barn door, even if his hips were ridiculously narrow. And those muscles! Did he belong to a gym somewhere? His body actually blocked out the sun.

Backing up two steps, she said tersely, "*I* am going to my room to shower and dress. After that, *I* am going to find a restaurant and treat myself to a decent, civilized breakfast. Then I am going to that shopping mall I passed yesterday to buy some food—and a coffeemaker. *You* are staying here. Any other questions, Mr. Logan?"

Gabe smiled and shook his head, his tousled dark hair falling over his forehead. "Nope. Not a single one. Just a small observation. Two, actually. One, I'll be more than happy to take care of Mandy while you're gone. And, two—you look almost human this morning, sweetheart, with your hair tumbling down around your shoulders like that. It's naturally blond, isn't it? If I were a *real* artist, I'd probably want to paint you. Now, if you would just lower your guard a little, we might just make this thing work."

"I'm *not* your sweetheart!" Erica shouted, wishing he would have the good sense to leave her alone. Her only other response was to loudly slam her bedroom door behind her—waking Mandy, whom Gabe had patted to sleep only ten minutes earlier.

As the infant's wails echoed through the suddenly quiet house, Erica's door opened a crack and she asked in a defeated voice, "That was my fault, wasn't it? I'll go to her."

"No way! You go get some breakfast, Ms. Fletcher," Gabe told her angrily, already heading for his niece's door. "Go somewhere that no one will look at you cockeyed when you crook your pinky as you sip your coffee. I wouldn't let you near Mandy right now on a bet. You'd just better come back here this afternoon at least outwardly resembling a rational human being and ready to go to work."

The last words Erica heard as she closed her door—quietly this time—also came from Gabe, his voice now low, gentle, soothing. "Hiya, sweetheart," he said, entering Amanda's room, "did that nasty lady scare you? Well, you just come to Uncle Gabe, and we'll sit in the big rocking chair and talk about it, okay? Mmm, don't you smell good, sweetheart? Uncle Gabe gave you a bath this morning, didn't he? He gave you a bath, and he washed your hair, and he fed you your bottle, and he—"

Erica leaned against her closed door, refusing to listen to more of "St. Gabriel's" self-serving horn-blowing, hating the smug, infuriating man with every ounce of her being.

"I never raise my voice," Erica mused as she drove out of the restaurant parking lot. "Never. I'm not hysterical. I am a calm, rational, reasonably intelligent person. I'm respected, even looked up to by my employees and business associates from Philadelphia to Hong Kong. So why am I letting that ridiculous man get under my skin?"

Erica had spent an hour in the restaurant, drinking three cups of coffee while she aimlessly pushed bacon and scrambled eggs around her plate and nibbled on a piece of buttered toast. Never a fan of big breakfasts, she had ordered the large meal out of spite, as if contrasting the substantial meal with the scarcity of food to be found in the Logan kitchen.

She had at last calmed her temper sufficiently to realize that she had behaved like a witch that morning—attacking Gabriel Logan the moment he had walked into the kitchen—but she still couldn't bring herself to believe that she was the only one at fault. After all, he had known she was coming; the least he could have done was order in some groceries.

Super-hoagies and French fries, indeed. If that was his idea of dinner, she'd better find a catering service first thing Monday morning. In the meantime, she still had the rest of the day to get through, and although catering her dinners seemed sensible, she had planned to fend for herself for breakfasts and lunches. She'd spent enough time in her Manhattan corporate condominium to know how to cook at least a rudimentary meal.

"But not in that depressing excuse for a kitchen," she declared, turning into the mall parking lot. "I'd probably get ptomaine poisoning. If this arrangement of ours is ever going to work, I'm going to have to buy some food—and a truckload of paper plates."

Erica's first stop at the mall was a small department store, where she quickly bought a coffeemaker, some canisters and an alarm clock. She hesitated over the alarm clock, already having learned that Amanda was a pretty good natural one, but she had hated having to search in the dark for her watch on the nightstand that morning to see what time it was.

Her next stop was at the supermarket that was a part of the complex. It was only Erica's second visit to a grocery store—her first visit having occurred a few days earlier when she'd been following Gabe—and unfortunately it showed.

She walked inside the store without first getting a shopping cart, so that she had to walk all the way around the checkout counters to get back outside, find a cart, and start over from the beginning.

She stood at the deli counter for five minutes, silently fuming at the way she was being ignored, before realizing that she'd have to take a number in order to be served. Yet once she was waited on, she found that she didn't know how much of anything to order.

In the end she bought two pounds of everything—Swiss cheese, baked ham, roast beef, potato salad and, considering it to be in the way of a peace offering, thinly sliced hard salami. The girl behind the counter confused Erica by telling her she hoped the "party" went well as she handed her three heavy bags of food.

A teenage clerk in the produce aisle yelled at Erica for sampling the strawberries without buying any, and she was nearly run over in the housewares aisle by a five-year-old boy pushing a fully loaded cart while making noises like a race car motor. With a new appreciation of the plight of housewives, she pushed on, now on the lookout for paper plates and plastic utensils.

Eventually she figured out which can of coffee to buy and found a wheat bread that didn't look as bad as the rest. She even bought three small bouquets of fresh flowers she planned to use to brighten up her bedroom, as well as several brightly colored kitchen towels. Satisfied at last, she pushed her extremely full cart to the checkout.

And that's when the trouble started.

"You're in the wrong lane, ma'am," the clerk told Erica after she had waited in line for several minutes. "This is the speedy checkout. I've got an eight-item limit. You have to go over there."

Erica looked to her left in disbelief. "Over there" was a large area loaded with carts that positively bulged with food. The sight of cranky toddlers, older children begging for candy, and angry adults holding defrosting cartons of ice cream did little to make Erica want to join them.

Surely there had to be another way.

Erica turned back to the frowning clerk, smiling her most professional smile as she reached for her purse. She had handled her share of maître d's; surely this couldn't be much different from that.

"I can't go over there, miss," she explained silkily. "There's no room, and I'm in such a hurry. I'm sure you can handle more than eight items. You look very competent." She reached into her wallet and pulled out a crisp ten-dollar bill, folding it discreetly before handing it to the clerk. "I'm sure we understand each other better now...."

"I said, I don't wish to discuss it anymore. And please get down from there, you're in my way. Were you raised in a barn or something? You look like a giant vulture searching for prey."

Gabe continued to sit on his perch atop the counter, watching as she unloaded the paper bags, slamming food and cleaning products onto the kitchen table. "Wow, chocolate-chip cookies. I like that brand, but homemade's better. My mother used to make them. They were all soft, and the chocolate chips were sort of gooey inside. Hey, you don't suppose—"

"No, Mr. Logan," Erica replied dispassionately. "I don't suppose. Now go away, please, let me get finished here. This kitchen is so cluttered that I don't know where to put anything."

"Ah, come on, Ms. Fletcher, finish the story for me. So, you handed the money to the clerk and she came out from behind the cash register and started loading the groceries onto the conveyor for you. I hope you gave her another tip, because they're not supposed to do that, you know. And then this 'huge' man holding a six-pack of diet soda started yelling at you. Then what?"

Erica stopped unloading the bags to stand staring at him, a frozen apple pie in one hand and a pack of paper towels in the other. "He had this huge belly," she said, shivering in distaste as she closed her eyes for a moment to conjure up a picture of the man. "He was wearing purple and green Bermuda shorts—and an undershirt. And black socks! I don't think he'd shaved in a week."

Gabe nodded. "Probably on vacation. Poor guy. All he wanted to do was grab himself some diet soda and get back to his overstuffed chair in time to watch the Phillies. They're playing a doubleheader at home today against the Cubs. You're lucky he didn't start a riot."

Frowning, Erica looked out the kitchen window. "He did start a riot," she informed him slowly. "Or at least a small one. He was extremely loud, and excessively rude." She shook her head. "Why aren't there curtains on this window?"

"They're in the wash," Gabe answered automatically, adding, "or at least I think they are. It's been so long, I forget. I didn't realize they weren't on the window. This guy, he didn't try to hurt you or anything, did he?" he asked, wishing he could have kept the sudden concern he felt for her out of his voice.

Erica closed her eyes, reliving those few embarrassing minutes before the store manager had come along to take charge, listening once more as the angry customer shouted to anyone who'd cared to know that "This dame here is trying to bribe her way through the express line." Before the manager could restore order by opening another checkout line, many of the customers had shown signs of turning into a mob.

"I handled it," was all she said, reaching into another grocery bag to pull out a large plastic deli bag. "Here," she said, tossing it to him. "I hope you really like salami. I should have ordered it by the slice, I guess. I think you could feed an army with this. Oh, that's Amanda, isn't it?"

Gabe shifted his attention from the gigantic mound of sliced salami in his hands to look at the kitchen clock. "It's Mandy, all right, and right on time. You finish putting your stuff away and I'll get her."

"Would you like, er, that is . . . I was going to make myself some lunch and, ah, well—"

"I'd love one, thank you," Gabe said genially, rescuing Erica from her garbled attempt at bridging the gap between them. "Salami on rye, with mustard, if you please."

"It's wheat, not rye," Erica corrected, holding up the loaf so he could see it. "The fiber, you know."

Mandy let out an indignant bellow, unused to being ignored. "Whatever," Gabe said, heading down the hall. "Get a bottle out of the refrigerator and run it under some hot water, will you? I'll get Mandy and meet you on the patio."

Ten minutes later, after changing Mandy's diaper and dressing her in a clean cotton undershirt, Gabe walked out onto the patio to see Erica placing a vase of fresh flowers in the center of the round picnic table. She stood back a moment, then carefully shifted the vase two inches to the left, tilting her head to inspect her work. He was surprised she didn't use a ruler to measure even more precisely. He'd never met a Type-A personality before, but he felt pretty sure he was looking at one now.

Green woven place mats Gabe didn't know he owned sat on either side of the table, covered with paper plates decorated in a green and white lattice design. Clear plastic cups, plastic utensils, and honest-to-goodness cloth napkins completed the place settings.

Gabe nodded his head in approval. "Looks nice," he said, lowering Mandy into her infant seat in a shaded area of the flagstone patio. "I tried the bottle, but she's not hungry yet. She was just wet. You know, I'd forgotten how a properly set table looks."

Erica smiled, flattered. "I found the place mats and napkins in the china cabinet in the dining room. I imagine they were your mother's. I hope you don't mind, but I just can't stand paper napkins."

Gabe shrugged. "I have to teach you how to use the washer and dryer anyway—to do Mandy's diapers."

Erica stopped in the midst of spooning deli potato salad onto her plate. "Diapers?" she squeaked. "Mandy—I mean, Amanda wears *cloth* diapers? Why?"

Gabe sat down and picked up half of his sandwich, eyeing the thick stack of salami between the pieces of wheat bread. "She's allergic to something in the paper ones. The perfume, I think. Dr. Halloran ordered cloth diapers. Hey, this looks good. When does the fleet get in to eat the rest of it?"

Racking her brain, desperate to find a way out of this latest problem—and ignoring Gabe's sarcastic remark—Erica asked hopefully, "Isn't there a single reputable diaper service around here? I'd be willing to pay for it, of course. I'm sure there must be something..."

Liking the look of dismay that had crossed Erica's normally serene features as much as he disliked this latest reference to her fat wallet, Gabe answered happily, "They've got chemicals in them, too. Disinfectants that give her a rash. Nope, around here we do diapers the old-fashioned way. We *wash* 'em."

"You're disgusting," Erica snapped, picking up her roast beef sandwich and taking a small bite. As she chewed, she looked down at her niece who was happily watching a butterfly wing its way across the yard. Her heart melted, again. "Is Amanda going to be awake for a while now?" she asked hopefully. "I've barely been able to spend any time with her."

Leaning back in his chair, Gabe seemed to consider her question. "The Phillies game starts in five minutes, and I'd sure like to catch a few innings. Tell you what—I'll get Mandy's bottle before she loses interest in the great outdoors, and you can feed her. Then you can spread a blanket under that small shady tree for her afternoon nap."

Suddenly all of Erica's fears were back in full force. Amanda was so little, so helpless—and she was so inexperienced! "You—you're going to leave me out here with her? Alone?"

Gabe allowed the chair to fall forward so that he could rise. "I've hidden your car keys, Ms. Fletcher. You wouldn't get far on foot. Thanks for the sandwich, but from now on I'll fend for myself. I've been all grown up for a lot of years. I'll feed Mandy for you, but only this one last time. From now on it's your ball game."

Erica leaped to her feet. "That's not what I mean, you suspicious bastard!" she shouted after him. "And you've got mustard stuck to your stupid mustache!" Her voice startled Amanda, who immediately began to cry, and Erica dropped her chin onto her chest. "That's twice in one day—and it's only lunchtime," she muttered, hating herself for allowing him to bait her.

She gathered Mandy carefully into her arms, kissing the baby's damp forehead and apologizing for having frightened her. Mandy quieted immediately, filling Erica with confidence that the feeding would go well.

"Here you go, Ms. Fletcher, one bottle of formula," Gabe said from the doorway. "I've changed my mind," he added, holding the bottle just out of her reach. "I think I should watch you, just to make sure you're doing it right."

"I did it Friday afternoon and again last night, didn't I?" Erica pointed out, bristling. "It doesn't take a Rhodes scholar to give a child a bottle. Go watch your Phillies, why don't you? If you're lucky, one of them might score a touchdown."

"That's football, Ms. Fletcher," Gabe pointed out, his lips twitching. It was nice to know she wasn't perfect all the time. "The Philadelphia Phillies are a Major League *baseball* team."

"I knew that," Erica snapped, quickly snatching the bottle from his hand while his guard was down and then sitting in the chair to begin feeding Mandy. "Someone I dated in college was a big Phillies fan, and I learned to enjoy the game myself. They won the World Series in 1980 and the National League pennant in 1983. They're a little soft when it comes to having a consistent long-ball hitter, but I still think they have a good shot at another pennant this year."

Gabe stared at her, his mouth hanging open. "Well, I'll be damned," he breathed at last. "Ms. Fletcher, you're full of surprises."

She smiled up at him, feeling better, more in control than she had in days. This might work. This whole ridiculous plan just might work after all. "Yes. I know. And you may call me Erica."

Chapter Five

A dozen freshly sharpened Number Two pencils sat waiting in a chipped coffee mug that had the words Damn I'm Good emblazoned on the side in orange letters.

A full set of shiny pen points, ranging in width from very fine to broad, were neatly lined up according to size in a plastic tray beside a half dozen full ink pots.

Thick matte drawing paper was clipped to the drawing board, its creamy white blankness yet to become acquainted with either the pencils or the pen points.

Perched precariously on a corner of the drawing table, a hollow-eyed skull grinned at the rest of the room, mocking the man standing in front of the window overlooking the backyard—the man who was supposed to be sitting in front of the drawing table, duplicating that skull down to its last missing tooth for a biological textbook.

Gabe had been in the small room he called his office since seven o'clock that morning, after tossing a load of diapers into the washing machine in the laundry room across the hallway. The only sound in this small wing of the ranch house was that of those same diapers, washed and rinsed twice and now whirling around in the clothes dryer.

It was eleven-thirty, nearly time for lunch, and those drying diapers were Gabe's singular accomplishment of the morning.

Resting his forehead against a cool pane of glass, Gabe sighed. He should be working. But how was he supposed to get anything done when Erica insisted upon lying on a blanket in the sun, wearing the most modestly indecent bathing suit he'd ever seen?

It was green, the same deep emerald color as her eyes, and it molded to Erica's long-lined curves like a second skin. Strapless, it didn't plunge in the front or dip in the back, and the leg openings were no more revealing than a pair of shorts. Yet Gabe had no trouble imagining the treasures that suit concealed and exposed at the same time. The suit was as sexy as the most daring bikini, even more alluring than if she had been lying in the sun nude.

"Well, almost as alluring," Gabe corrected, smiling at the thought, watching as Erica raised a hand to sweep her long, unbound blond hair away from her nape as she turned onto her stomach. Mandy still dozed beside her in the shade. "The woman is perfect, a sculptor's masterpiece brought to life. I don't think she has a single freckle, or even one small mole."

He sniffed derisively, shaking his head. "She probably wouldn't allow it," he decided ruefully, remembering Erica's passion for perfection. In the week that she had been living in his house, sleeping in his mother's room, Erica Fletcher had managed to put her stamp of order and neatness on everything from the spice cabinet in the kitchen to the bookshelves in the family room.

There were the flowers, for one thing. Unearthing vases from cabinets Gabe had never bothered opening, she had filled the house with the color and beauty and heady smell of cut flowers. Even his bedroom wasn't off limits when it came to finding another empty tabletop to serve as a base for her artistically arranged blooms.

Reaching up to rub his chest, which was covered with a thin plaid cotton shirt thanks to Erica's silent but understood disdain for the sight of his bare skin at the breakfast table, Gabe admitted to himself that the house hadn't looked so much like a home since his mother had been alive.

White organdy curtains now hung at the living-room windows, curtains Gabe vaguely remembered seeing there years before, and the kitchen curtains were finally back in place. Gary had been a bit of an eccentric, Gabe admitted silently, redecorating the place all in brown, but the curtains certainly helped to rid the place of its institutional atmosphere. Nevertheless, the changes bothered him.

Erica had very sweetly asked his permission before doing anything, yet each change, each small alteration, had made Gabe feel like he was losing ground, losing control over his own life.

And it wasn't only the house. Erica was taking over with Mandy, too.

Gabe watched as Erica stood up, slipping into a peach-colored lace wrap that barely skimmed the top of her hips before reaching down to confidently lift the now awake Mandy into her arms. She handled the child with ease, kissing the top of Mandy's head before walking toward the back door in her bare feet.

Obviously her reliable inner clock had told her that it was lunchtime, Gabe thought, knowing that in less than a half hour she'd be calling him to come sit down at the table on the patio where he'd find yet another thick salami sandwich waiting for him.

"God, how I hate salami," he swore, turning away from the window to glare at the skull that seemed to condemn him for complaining. After all, what grounds for complaint did he have?

His house was being run smoothly, effortlessly, for the first time since he had moved back after Gary's death. The kitchen was as spotless as his mother had always prided herself on keeping it, and there were no longer weird foodstuffs taking on lives of their own inside the refrigerator.

He was served a different, delicious gourmet meal every night, not that Erica prepared it herself, and he had even gone to the movie theater at the local mall one evening now that there was someone else in the house to take care of Mandy.

To take care of Mandy.

"Ah, yes," he grousingly told the skull, "and therein lies the rub, Bub."

Erica was taking care of Mandy. Oh, yes, indeedy, she certainly was! She was taking brilliant, flawless, faultless, loving care of his niece.

Gabe's biggest complaint about Ms. Erica Fletcher was that he had no complaints about her. Any thoughts he may have had about Erica having merely stepped into her father's already comfortable shoes at

F and W and then playing at being a hardworking executive had faded within twenty-four hours of her arrival at the house on Beaver Valley Road.

She was good, he conceded, looking at his coffee mug turned pencil holder. She was *damn* good. He had come into the kitchen the other night just as she had received one of the dozen telephone calls she'd already had from Philadelphia. While he had pretended not to listen, she'd swiftly dealt with at least ten problems that had cropped up in her absence. She had been fair, she thought fast on her feet, and she didn't knock the guy on the other end of the telephone over the head with her orders. She was a professional, through and through.

As a matter of fact, since that incident in the checkout line at the supermarket, she hadn't taken another false step. He'd even found a child care book in the dining room with several key passages highlighted in yellow ink.

She was in his house for the long haul, willing to work hard, determined to succeed. Determined to take Mandy away with her. Away from him. It would all be very legal, very right and tight and proper. And he should know, for he had signed that damnable contract she'd had her Philadelphia lawyer draw up for her.

Gabe didn't know whether he wanted to kiss her for being so smart, or slug her—for being so smart.

Picking up the skull, Gabe collapsed into his padded swivel chair, leaning back as he studied the grinning head. "Alas, poor Yorick! I knew him—

"'Here hung those lips that I have kissed I know not how oft. Where be your gibes now? Your gambols, your songs, your flashes of merriment that were wont to set the table on a roar? Not one now to mock your own grinning?' *Hamlet*. Act Five, I believe. I always liked that part. Shakespeare had a sense of humor, even when he was being macabre. Amanda's had her lunch, the little love, and I've put her down for a nap. Your lunch is waiting for you on the patio.''

Gabe nearly toppled out of his chair as, her recitation over, Erica walked into the room, still dressed in her bathing suit. She had never come into his office before, always knocking on the door and calling her message through the wood. "You read Shakespeare?" he asked blankly, staring at the emerald-green swimsuit through the holes in the creamy peach lace.

Erica nodded as she circled the room, studying the pen-and-ink drawings that lined the walls. Without asking permission, she moved closer to one particular arrangement of drawings.

"These aren't for textbooks," she said, staring at finely detailed renderings of faces, faces that ranged from a defeated old man wearing a three-day growth of beard to a small drawing of Mandy, asleep, one chubby finger stuck in her mouth. "Why, Gabe, you lied to me. You're extremely talented. These drawings, they—they're *exquisite!*"

Gabe's gaze shifted quickly to the small table beside him and he reached out to turn over the sketchbook that was lying there. They had come so far in a single week; they had actually graduated from merely being civil to each other to making the first overtures of friendship. The last thing he wanted was for Erica to retreat into her brittle shell again, away from him.

But it was too late; Erica had already seen the sketchbook.

She picked it up, staring at the topmost page for a long time before a faint flush of color entered her smooth cheeks. "This is supposed to be me, isn't it?" she asked, looking straight at Gabe, clearly daring him to look away. "Of course it is. I don't know why I'm asking the question. I-it's very good."

Gabe rushed into speech. "Erica, please, let me explain. It's not at all what you're thinking..."

Placing the sketchbook back on the table with exaggerated care, Erica slowly turned and headed for the open doorway. When she spoke again, her voice was cool and clipped. "How could you possibly presume to know what I'm thinking, Mr. Logan?"

"Damn it, Erica, don't go all Mainline Matron on me!" Gabe protested, hopping to his feet. "You asked if I was an artist and I told you I wasn't. I'm not— yet—at least not in my own mind. I've only had one real showing, six months ago in New York. If a 'real' artist had drawn that you'd think nothing of it. That drawing would be art, right?"

"From the neck up that drawing might be art, Mr. Logan," Erica responded, turning to face him. "However, from the neck down, it is nothing more than speculation."

Suddenly, Gabe smiled. "Really? I thought I had judged the proportions fairly well. But if you want to set me straight where I went wrong, I'd be more than happy to have you pose for me sometime. As you can see—" he continued, pointing to the skull "—most of my subjects don't have the option of complaining when I haven't captured them just right."

Erica looked daggers at him, emerald-green daggers that warmed his blood even as he felt their sting in the pit of his stomach. "You're disgusting," she bit out, her chin raised in censure. "Completely disgusting."

Gabe returned her stare, allowing his gaze to rake her from head to foot and back again. "And you've got the greatest legs I've ever seen."

"It's not my legs that we're discussing, Mr. Logan," Erica pointed out, blushing as her words revealed her thoughts.

Walking toward her, Gabe smiled, saying softly, "No, it's not, is it? And you know what, Ms. Erica Fletcher? I don't think you're angry because my drawing is wrong. You're angry because it's right."

"N-no, i-it's not that," Erica fumbled, taking a quick step backward as he came within six inches of her, still smiling down at her, his intentions showing clearly in his eyes. "It's just...it's just that—"

Erica stopped speaking as Gabe's hand reached out to stroke her cheek. "So soft, so smooth. Your skin is like warm marble, Erica. Warm, living marble with the kiss of the sun on it. You smell like sunshine, too. Sunshine and clover and lilacs. You fascinate me. What do you taste like, Erica? Do you taste like summertime, too?"

Gabe concentrated on her lips, seeing them move but not hearing a word she said. Her lips were moist. Inviting. Irresistible. He swallowed hard, knowing he was taking a step that might lead them both into disaster, then lowered his mouth to cover hers.

Slanting his mouth against hers, he could feel the stiffness in her relaxing until her lips parted on a sigh, allowing him to deepen the kiss. As his arms closed around her slim waist he could feel the weight of her breasts against his chest, and the length of her perfect legs against the front of his thighs.

"Oh, Erica," he breathed into her unbound hair, breaking the kiss to hold her tightly against him. "You're driving me insane, do you know that? You're the most infuriating, complicated, unnerving woman—all I can do is think about you...want you...need you...."

Her arms no longer hung at her sides but held him firmly to her as her fingertips bit into his back. She tipped her head, allowing him to press kisses against the side of her throat, wordlessly giving him access to her body.

Gabe couldn't think anymore, couldn't begin to weigh the consequences of his actions. All he knew was that the woman in his house had somehow become the woman in his arms, and he wanted her more than he had ever wanted anything in his life.

Slowly, nervous beyond measure, he moved his hands lower, until at last they fit beneath the hem of her lace wrap. Then he skimmed back up the sides of her rib cage with his fingertips.

Her hands lifted higher, grasping his shoulders, caressing his neck. Erica was sending out signals; signals he was receiving loud and clear. She wasn't fighting him. This was surrender, and he knew it.

Raising his head, Gabe looked into her face, at her closed eyes, her slightly parted lips. With a groan, he claimed her mouth once more. His tongue reached out, skimming her soft inner lips before plunging into her mouth, where it was welcomed without reserve.

How it happened he did not know, could not remember, but somehow his hands pushed the lace wrap away and found their way inside the strapless bathing suit, to cup the firm flesh waiting for him there. His artist's fingers told him his drawing had not been the result of wishful thinking, but the realization of his fondest dreams.

She was more than the beautiful, perfect creature he had imagined. She was flesh and blood and sweet, throbbing desire. And she was his. She was all his.

And then, suddenly, the hands that had drawn him to her so sweetly were forcefully pushing him away.

A moment later Gabe was alone. He stood very still for a long minute, wondering why he had thought the rich, beautiful, *perfect* Erica Fletcher might feel about him the way he knew he was beginning to feel about her—and then he picked up one of the ink pots and flung it against the wall.

Erica sat in the darkened movie theater, staring at the screen. It was a teenage horror movie. She liked musicals, or spy stories. Even cartoons. She hated horror movies. She ought to get up and leave.

An hour passed, during which some disfigured creature in a ski mask killed off more than a dozen screaming teenagers in ways that ranged from sickening to laughable, and still Erica sat slumped in her seat, staring at the screen without really seeing it.

How could I have allowed things to go so far? she asked herself, not for the first time. *How could I have actually encouraged him to kiss me, to touch me, to*—

Erica shook her head, refusing to think about the liberties she had granted Gabe, the advances she had given him every reason to believe she would welcome. And she *had* welcomed them. At least she refused to lie to herself and pretend she had been disgusted by his actions, or merely bored by them.

Gabriel Logan was an accomplished lover, Erica was sure of that. He was so tall, so handsome, so very easy on the eyes. With that silly mustache and that naughty-little-boy look on his face, he must be able to get women into his bed without even exerting himself.

Why, she had practically seduced herself, Erica decided, knowing that she had been flattered by the pen-and-ink drawing he had made of her. *The drawing!* Erica bolted upright in the seat, knocking her uneaten tubful of popcorn onto the floor. She had forgotten about the drawing. It was still in his office.

How long had she been sitting here? Erica glanced at her wrist but it was too dark in the theater to see her watch. After hiding out in her bedroom all afternoon, she had driven to the mall, to eat a hot dog she didn't want and walk aimlessly through several stores before at last deciding to lose herself in a dark movie theater. Amanda would be all right. Gabe would take care of her. Gabe could take care of anything. Besides, he had gone out to the movies one night, hadn't he? It was only fair that she could do the same.

But now it was nearly eleven o'clock. She stood up and headed for the aisle. She had to get home. She had to get that drawing!

On the short trip back to Beaver Valley Road, Erica forced herself to concentrate on her driving, even remembering to buckle her seat belt, but quick flashes of Gabe's sketch kept appearing in the headlights of oncoming cars to haunt her.

It was a beautiful drawing, she knew, and a flattering likeness. He had sketched her sitting in the sun, her legs drawn up beside her as she leaned back on her hands, her face thrown up to the sky, her hair falling down around her shoulders, fanning out in a slight breeze.

And I'm not wearing a stitch of clothing! she screamed inside her head. He'd gracefully captured the flare of her right hip, and the smooth curve of her waist. But what he did to her breasts—the way he made them look as if they were budding flowers, lifting themselves to the sun— "Oh, boy, does Gabe really see me like that? Me, the ugly duckling of the Fletcher clan? The corporate leader, the consummate businesswoman? He made me look almost beautiful."

Erica pulled into the driveway, cutting the headlights before they could play across the sliding doors in the family room and alert Gabe that she was home. Hunting in her purse for the key he had given her for the front door the day she'd arrived, she quietly crept into the darkened house and tiptoed down the hall to his office.

The drawing was gone. She looked everywhere, even in the drawers of the file cabinet behind his drawing table, but the picture was nowhere to be found. "He probably sent it out to be framed, the bastard," she said ruefully, at last giving up the search.

Wearily, she sat in his chair, staring at the spot where they had stood together earlier. She closed her eyes, reliving those heady moments in his arms. Ever since their first angry kiss, Erica had known she was attracted to Gabriel Logan, but it had taken the events of that afternoon to show her that he was attracted to her, as well.

No, not attracted. That was too mild a word. Gabriel Logan wanted her.

She bowed her head, hating herself. *And you want him. Cool, unflappable, untouchable Erica Fletcher wants Gabriel Logan so much that she made an absolute fool of herself over the man.*

"I'm as bad as Meredith," she murmured out loud, addressing the grinning skull. "I never gave a single thought to Amanda while Gabe was kissing me, not one single thought. What am I trying to do? Am I trying to become a good aunt for Amanda or am I trying to seduce her uncle?"

"If you want my opinion, I think you're trying to drive yourself crazy. You can't answer you, you know. Where in blazes have you been?"

Erica's head shot up as Gabe's words reached her and she saw him lounging in the doorway, his dark hair tousled, his face flushed as if he had been sleeping. He seemed to have lost his shirt again, as he was clad only in a pair of running shorts, and he had a strange look on his face, almost as if he was worried about something. And he had heard what she said—or at least he'd heard part of it. If she was smart, she'd pretend that he hadn't heard enough to know what she had been saying.

It didn't occur to Erica that he could have been worried about her. Instead, immediately Erica's thoughts left her own problems as she asked, "Is Amanda all right? Please forgive me for leaving her this afternoon. It's only that I knew you were here and, well, I just felt the need to get away by myself for a few hours. She didn't give you any trouble, did she?"

Gabe crossed his arms over his bare chest and Erica swallowed hard as she watched the quick rippling of the muscles in his arms. Those arms had held her against him only a few hours earlier. Those hands had caressed her, those long, slender fingers had teased her. Her stomach did a small flip.

He shrugged, dismissing her fears if not her traitorous thoughts. "She wasn't too crazy about her rice cereal tonight, but she and I managed to muddle through without you. Are you all right?"

She looked at him, really seeing him for the first time. Why hadn't she ever noticed the keen intelligence in his midnight-blue eyes, or the soft fullness of his mouth beneath that ridiculous, wonderful mustache? "I—I'm fine, just, er *fine*. And you?"

Pushing himself away from the doorjamb, Gabe crossed the room to stand on the other side of his drawing table, his face solemn. "I've been better. What did I do wrong, Erica? Did I scare you? I didn't mean to come on quite so strong, you know. It's just that, well, you're really some woman. One minute you were trading insults and the next . . ." His voice trailed off as he picked up the skull, idly shifting it from hand to hand. "Anyway, I didn't mean to frighten you. It won't happen again."

Erica pressed her fingers to her forehead, trying to gather her thoughts. If she told him that he hadn't frightened her, that she had frightened herself, what would he think? She couldn't honestly tell him that she'd never wish for him to repeat his actions, yet she knew that if he touched her now she would literally fall apart.

"Erica?" Gabe prompted, leaning closer. "Are we still on speaking terms?"

Drawing on all her years of practice, and putting on a brave face, Erica smiled up at him, her stiff cheeks hurting with the effort. "Don't be ridiculous, Gabe.

Of course we're still speaking. This afternoon was, well, it was like the song says—just one of those things. I'm really more angry with myself than I am with you. You're a man, you took what was offered. I just wouldn't want you to think that I—'' she stumbled for the words. "That I'm, er, I'm—''

"Like Meredith?" he finished for her, his voice gentle. "I heard you mention her name as I came in.''

Erica's eyes filled with tears. He *had* heard her. So much for subtlety. "Yes,'' she admitted, "like Meredith.'' She turned her head away. "God, I feel so disloyal. She was my sister and—''

"You loved her.'' Gabe walked around the drawing table and put his hand on her shoulder. Erica felt his touch and had to bite her bottom lip to hold back a sob. "She was your sister, Erica. I wouldn't have much respect for you if you didn't care about her. You're a lady, through and through, and I respect you, old-fashioned as that sounds.''

"Gabe, I—''

"No more talk tonight, okay?" Gabe patted her shoulder and then walked toward the door. "Why don't you go get a good night's sleep and in the morning we'll start over again, as if we're meeting for the first time, with nothing between us but our love for Mandy.''

"I do love her, Gabe," Erica called after him. "I love her more than I ever thought it was possible to love anybody. I'd do anything for her.''

Gabe turned in the doorway and directed a long stare at her. "Yes, Erica, I know. So would I. I'd do anything but give her up. Good night.''

After a few minutes had passed, when she was sure she wouldn't meet him in the hallway, Erica went to

her bedroom, Gabe's words echoing inside her head.
What had he meant by that last statement? They had
an agreement. A legal, binding agreement. A stupid,
insane, inane, impossible legal agreement! How she
wished she had never had that contract drawn up in
the first place. How could Gabe be attracted to her,
want to kiss her, when with every passing day, each
hour gotten through without incident, the time she
would take Amanda away with her was drawing
nearer, ever nearer. How could she do it? How could
she take Amanda away from Gabe, separate Gabe
from his beloved niece? How could she do such a thing
and still live with herself?

*That's what comes from living your life with your
eye always on the result, the win, the next project,* she
told herself ruefully. She had tackled gaining custody
of Amanda with all her usual drive, her unflagging
energy—her inbred fear of failure, of not living up to
expectations. She had proved her father wrong,
proved everyone wrong, by becoming a competent—
no, more than competent—a *great* CEO of F and W.
If she was an overachiever, she had come by it honestly.

And now, following a lifelong pattern, she had accepted Gabe's challenge. Not content to simply master the care of Amanda, she had taken on the running
of the entire Logan household, determined to do everything, and do it better than anyone else had ever
done it.

Only she hadn't counted on the human element, the
Mandy Factor. She hadn't counted on the instant,
fierce, irrevocable bond of love that would bind her to
her sister's child from the moment she first set eyes on
the child. Gabe felt that same bond, that same fierce

protectiveness, that same overwhelming love. How could he not?

So once again she had to ask herself: how could she take Amanda away from a man who appeared to love her enough to put his own life on hold for twenty years in order to raise her?

How could she hurt Gabe, who had begun to mean more to her own personal happiness than she would ever admit?

Her head aching, Erica walked through her darkened bedroom to wash her face in the bathroom before getting undressed. At last, turning on the overhead light to find her nightgown, she saw the large white paper lying on the bed.

The drawing.

She walked over to look at it, hoping she'd find some answers to Gabe's feelings for her in the sketch. It was just as she remembered it, except for one startling change that confused her even more.

The figure in the sketch was now wearing a strapless bathing suit.

Chapter Six

"Here you are. It's such a nice morning, I thought you would have been on the patio. I'd like to talk to you about your sketches, if you don't mind." Erica's voice was a little too cheerful, a little too loud.

Gabe looked up from the sports section to see her standing in front of him, balancing Mandy on her hip. The child was fresh from her bath and dressed in a smocked white cotton dress dotted with tiny pink rosebuds. "Hiya, Princess," he greeted the infant. "Don't you look pretty. And, sorry—I *do* mind," he added, his voice an octave deeper, before returning his attention to last night's box scores.

"You're going to ignore me, aren't you, hoping I'll go away? Well, I won't. I'm not going to make this easy for you," she warned, taking another step toward him.

"What's that? Sorry, I wasn't listening. Hey, the Phillies won again. They're on a real streak—this makes one in a row."

"It's still early in the season. Wait until the All-Star break before you write them off," Erica answered automatically. She remained where she was, gnawing on her bottom lip as she decided on another course of action. "All right," she said at last. "But if we can't discuss your sketches, perhaps we can talk about the oils I found this morning in your room."

Gabe's head jerked up as he threw the newspaper down without bothering to fold it. "What in hell were you doing in my room? There are so many flowers in there now, when I'm in bed I don't know whether I'm going to sleep or being laid out for a public viewing. Damn it, Erica, why can't you mind your own business?"

She had known he might prove stubborn. Actually, had she been a betting person, she would have laid odds on it. That was why she had brought Mandy into the family room with her—as a sort of protection against his anger. She used the child now, shamelessly. "Stop growling like a bear with a sore head, Gabe. Can't you see you're upsetting the child?"

As the "child" was busily sticking the fingers of both hands in her mouth and gurgling happily at the red lamp shade across the room, Gabe merely arched his eyebrows and said, "Oh, yeah. Right. Poor child. Do you think I might have stunted her emotional growth? Shooting's too good for me!"

Longing to give him a good kick in the shins, Erica settled for a verbal attack. "You're just a coward, aren't you?" she asked, nodding her head as if in answer to her own question.

"A coward? You're hiding behind a three-month-old infant, and *you're* calling *me* a coward?"

Erica lifted her chin. "Yes, I'm calling you a coward. How old are you, Gabe, twenty-eight, thirty?"

"Thirty-two," he answered shortly. "And don't try to butter me up. I know a 'feminine wile' when it slaps me in the face."

"Right," Erica pushed on, sensing that she was getting through to him in spite of his protests. Last night, lying awake in her bed yet again, thinking, she had made up her mind to push Gabe back into the world. After all, they shared the care of Amanda now. She still phoned the office three or more times a day—there was no reason Gabe couldn't take some time to try becoming the artist she was sure he wanted to be. "You're thirty-two years old and you're behaving like a child who's afraid to show his drawings to the teacher. You're talented, Gabe, really talented. Why do you insist on hiding your work while you draw muscles and skulls like some sort of biological draftsman?"

"As I seem to recall telling you before, I had a showing in New York six months ago, Ms. Fletcher," Gabe countered, rising to glare into her eyes. "I hardly call that hiding."

Erica sniffed. "Yes, I know. I had one of my secretaries check it out. A small gallery in the Village. You call that a showing?"

Now Gabe was really angry. Maybe she was pressing too hard too soon. There were times she wished she wasn't such a "bottom line" person. But she had started this and she was going to finish it. She hugged Amanda a little closer.

"I call that a beginning, Ms. Fletcher," Gabe pointed out tightly. "We don't all have your connections, you know. Besides, the Metropolitan was all booked up for the season. They were displaying some other unknown—a Leonardo somebody-or-other."

Plunking Mandy into her infant seat, Erica stood and placed one hand on her hip. Lifting her right hand, she rubbed her thumb and index finger together in front of his face. "See this? It's the world's smallest violin, playing just for you. Poor baby, how I pity you."

Gabe took hold of her hand and pushed it down to her side. "You like living dangerously, lady?"

"Give me some credit, Gabe! I didn't say you could start at the top. But this is my business, or at least a good part of it. I judge art every day—paintings, sculptures, tapestries, antique furniture. Your work is exemplary. I'm not suggesting that your name should be a household word by now, that's wishful thinking. I'm only saying that your career should be on the upswing." She returned his angry glare in full measure, and went for broke. "I repeat. You're a coward."

"Why, Erica? Why all this interest?"

Sitting down on the floor next to Mandy, Erica tucked her cotton skirt around her bent knees, carefully searching for the right words to answer him. If she told him that she wanted to help him because she cared for him, she'd be admitting more than she wanted him to know. "You're Amanda's uncle," she offered at last, purposely avoiding his eyes.

Gabe slapped his open palm against his forehead. "Ah, now I get it. *Amanda Fletcher* can't have just *anybody* for a relative. Is that it?"

"No, that's not it!" Erica shouted, startling Mandy, whose bottom lip began to quiver. "Why don't you let me finish before attacking me? All I meant was that no matter how happy you were with your life before Amanda, you owe her the best possible future. I know your work commands a good rate, but the money is nothing compared to what you could earn if you devoted yourself completely to art, both your pen and inks and your oils. You've made a start. Don't let taking care of Amanda put an end to your career."

Gabe dropped into a chair, rubbing at his temples. "Let me get this straight, okay? As our arrangement stands, you'll be taking over Mandy in a little under two weeks. Obviously, you won't let her starve—"

"No!" Erica broke in, knowing where he was headed and unable to stop him from coming to the wrong conclusion—again.

"So, if it isn't money that Mandy needs from me," he continued, his voice hard, "then it's something else. Could that something else be fame? No, Fletchers don't actively seek fame, do they? But if I were to become rich and famous there would be a lot of demands on my time, wouldn't there? Why, I'd hardly be able to see Mandy. You'd have her all to yourself."

"You're being ridiculous!" Erica protested hotly.

Gabe's voice rose to bury hers. "And you're a royal pain in the—"

In her infant seat, Mandy let go of her stockinged toes to let out a bloodcurdling scream, stopping both adults in their tracks.

"Now look what you've done!" they accused each other in unison before Gabe snatched up his niece and stormed from the room, leaving Erica to glare after

them, her green eyes moist as she wondered how she'd
ever get him to listen to her.

Erica was loading the dishwasher as Gabe came into
the kitchen. He stopped just inside the door to lean
against the counter, enjoying watching her work. She
did everything so meticulously, rinsing each dish with
scalding water until he wondered if putting it into the
dishwasher was really necessary.

For the first few days they had eaten their meals
from paper plates, but Erica didn't seem to enjoy the
experience, and soon dirty dishes were piling up in the
double sink. He was going to wash them—eventually,
when there were enough there to make it worth his
while—but she had gotten to them first.

After making herself very clear on the fact that she
was in the house only to care for Mandy and not to act
as his personal maid, she had done a complete about-
face and taken over the running of the house lock,
stock and barrel. He had even found her running the
vacuum cleaner the other day. He wondered if she was,
as his mother had been, a "neat freak," or whether
she had a strong need to be in control.

No matter what it was, he liked it. He felt comfortable in a clean house, more comfortable than he had
during his bachelor days. His *bachelor* days? What
was he thinking? He was still a bachelor, still free to
come and go as he pleased. Free to date, free to dream,
free to— Oh, who was he kidding?

He was married. Married and the father of a three-
month-old daughter. That's how it felt, that's how it
would look to anyone peeking in through the kitchen
window.

That's how he liked to think of the three of them
when he was alone, late at night, longing to leave his
lonely bed and crawl in beside Erica, to lie with his
body pressed against her back, his arm around her
waist, listening to her slow, even breathing. She'd
wake, sensing his presence, and turn toward him, a
slow smile of welcome on her face. He'd return her
smile, then dip his head toward hers as his hand moved
to cup her—

He shook his head, banishing the image, to concentrate on Erica as she wet a dishcloth and began
wiping off the countertops. Her entire concentration
seemed centered on the task as she vigorously rubbed
at a coffee stain. "Erica?" he prompted quietly.
"Mandy's sound asleep and should be for another two
hours. Do you think we could talk now? I promise not
to shout anymore."

Her hand frozen in the act of wiping away some
bread crumbs, Erica turned her head to look at him.
"When you say 'talk,' Gabe, do you mean as in two
people sitting down to exchange ideas in conversation, or do you mean *you* talk and *I* listen?"

Walking over to take her hand, tossing the dishcloth into the sink, Gabe led her out onto the patio. "I
mean, we take turns. First I talk and you listen, and
then you talk and I listen. Fair enough?"

"You're wearing a shirt," Erica pointed out as she
sat down at the picnic table across from him, trying to
ease the tension between them after their argument
that morning. "This must be serious."

"It is," he agreed solemnly, then he rose once more.
"Iced tea. I should get you some iced tea."

Erica bent her head to hide a smile. He was nervous. Gabriel Logan was nervous about talking to her.

"I just had some, thank you anyway. Why don't you just start talking, Gabe?"

He nodded, but then sat quietly as he tried to understand why he was doing this. He was a private person, a very private person, and this was none of her business. But she had called him a coward, and he didn't want her to think of him that way. Not her. Not Erica.

"I was six years older than Gary," he began, easing himself into his explanation. "There were only the two of us. Dad worked as a pipe fitter and Mom stayed at home—making fudge and wearing gingham aprons. Gary and I both played in Little League, had picnics on the Lehigh Parkway and blew out the candles stuck into homemade chocolate cakes on our birthdays."

Erica spared a moment to think of her own home life, her growing up years spent mostly with servants or with other daughters of wealthy men at exclusive boarding schools. "It sounds nice," she said, meaning it.

"It was nice," Gabe agreed, smiling at his memories. "When he was nine, Gary discovered ice skating. He was consumed by it, and he was very, very good. By the time I was in my last year of art college he was living away from home for most of the year, training with a former Olympic champion in Vermont."

"Yes, I saw the photographs and newspaper clippings in an album in your parents' room. The judges certainly admired his style," Erica broke in, remembering one article in particular that praised Gary's original choreography.

Gabe's smile faded. "Then Dad died, and it looked as if Gary's dream would die with him."

Erica was embarrassed. Embarrassed and ashamed. She could tell where this story was leading. "Gabe," she interrupted, "you don't have to go on, honestly. I can see now how wrong I was."

Gabe looked out over the backyard, his expression pensive. "Professor Garvey said I was a fool to 'sacrifice' myself so that my brother could carve figure eights in a block of ice, but then he liked my work."

"Gary wasn't Professor Garvey's younger brother," Erica pointed out. "He was more concerned about you—and your talent."

"Yes, I know. But it takes a lot of years to establish yourself in the art world, Erica, while a good detail copyist makes a comfortable living from the word go."

Erica blinked back sudden tears. Gabe had given up his own promising future to help his brother. He must have loved him very much. Erica couldn't remember making any sacrifices for Meredith, not that Meredith would have asked her.

"You should have seen my mother's face the night Gary won his bronze medal." He stared straight at her as he ended, "You know, Erica, I wouldn't change what I did, not one minute of it. I'm still going to make it in the art world—I'll just be the world's oldest rookie, that's all. I've made a start, and Mandy won't always need constant attention."

Erica dropped her head into her hands, rubbing at her stinging eyes. Her first impression of Gabriel Logan had been the right one. He was a "nice" man. He had given up his dream because of his brother, not once, but twice, and all she could do was call him a coward. She felt terrible.

What she didn't feel was hopeless. She was Erica Fletcher, of F and W Import-Export, connected with some of the finest galleries in the world. She could help make up for the lost years, if only Gabe would let her. The door to success might still be marked Push, but everybody knew that on the other side of that door was the word Pull. It couldn't hurt! Her heart pounding with excitement, she looked up, only to see the silent warning on Gabe's face.

He hadn't come crawling to her when his brother died, begging her to take his fatherless niece off his hands so that he could get on with his life, nor had he accepted money in exchange for the child. He was a proud man. A good, proud, decent man.

And she loved him.

She felt her stomach drop to her toes. She, Erica Fletcher, a woman who prided herself on her level head, had fallen in love with a man she had known only two weeks. It was staggering!

"Okay," Gabe said, breaking into her thoughts just as Erica believed she would blurt out her feelings, ruining everything. "It's your turn."

"I—I," she stammered, wildly searching for something to say as she stood, ready to make her escape. "I just wanted to know if you wanted to play at being chef and cook steaks on the grill tomorrow. It's the Fourth of July, you know, and the caterer has the day off."

And then, while he stared at her quizzically, she turned on her heels and ran for the safety of the laundry room.

* * *

They were so careful around each other, even more careful than they had been those first days after their interlude in his office. They confined their conversations to Mandy, or the weather, or the fact that the Philadelphia Phillies had now won three games in a row.

Anything but what was on their minds—or in their hearts.

On Wednesday Gabe decided to offer an olive branch of sorts, telling Erica that he was going out for a round of golf and then dinner with an old friend and that she could take Mandy to the pediatrician alone.

"The appointment's set for four o'clock. Dr. Halloran's a good man. You'll like him," he told a bemused Erica as he lifted a set of golf clubs onto his shoulder and headed for the door. "I already called and told the nurse you'd be bringing Mandy for her regular monthly checkup today. Don't worry about a thing."

Erica longed to throw her arms around his neck and kiss him. He hadn't said it out loud, but he was telling her that he trusted her. He trusted her not to pack up Mandy's things and take the child to Philadelphia while he was gone. "I'll be very careful with her," she promised solemnly, walking Gabe to his car.

"I know that," Gabe answered, reaching into the back of his car for Mandy's infant carrier. He had already given Erica detailed directions to the doctor's office. "I'll just put this crazy contraption into your car for you. Do you know how it works?"

Erica looked at the infant seat and nodded dumbly. It had more straps on it than her wear-it-any-way bra, but she wasn't about to say anything that might keep her from having this time alone with her niece. "I'll figure it out," she assured him, lifting her chin.

And she would, Gabe knew. This was a woman who could figure out anything—except the fact that he was rapidly falling head over heels in love with her. After loading his golf clubs into the trunk, he turned and looked around the driveway, suddenly nervous. "Well, I guess that's it," he announced, spreading his arms. "Aren't you going to wish me luck as I go off to do battle with sand traps and foot-long rough?"

Erica dipped her head, smiling. "You make it sound as if you're going off to war," she teased. "Remember, it's only a game."

Gabe walked over and laid his hands on her shoulders. "You wouldn't say that if you knew Jim Matthews, my opponent. He's a real blood-and-guts golfer. I'll be lucky to make it back home to my two ladies alive."

Erica blushed, loving the offhand way he had referred to Mandy and herself. "In that case, I guess I'll have to wish you luck," she said, looking up at him to see his blue eyes twinkling mischievously.

"I was hoping you'd say that," Gabe admitted as he swiftly lowered his head to capture her lips in a swift, hard kiss.

As he backed the car out of the driveway, Erica stood watching him, her fingers pressed to her lips, her heart pounding hopefully as she dared to dream.

"Oh, Amanda, darling, please don't cry any more. Please, sweetheart."

It was seven o'clock and Mandy had been crying nonstop for more than an hour. The nurse had told Erica that the baby might react to her second of a se-

ries of routine immunization shots, but the woman's
warning had not prepared Erica for this. Nothing she
did satisfied Mandy for more than a few moments,
and Erica had tried everything; rocking her, carrying
her, offering her a bottle, even singing to her. But
Amanda was still wailing, and Erica was at the end of
her rope.

Her dinner, delivered an hour earlier by the catering service, was still sitting untouched on the kitchen
table, the roast beef soaking in congealed gravy. It had
been impossible to try to eat with Mandy sobbing into
her shoulder.

As she paced back and forth in Mandy's bedroom,
Erica alternately cursed Gabe for spending a day with
his friend, leaving her to cope alone with a baby he
knew would be cranky and wished with all her might
that he'd come home to rescue her before she started
crying, too.

But no, she told herself, softly crooning into Mandy's ear as the child continued to sob. She didn't really want him to come home now and see how
woefully inept she was at handling this small crisis. It
wasn't as if Mandy was really sick; she didn't even
have a fever. She was merely having a mild reaction to
the shot. Within another few hours everything would
be just fine. The last thing Erica wanted to do was
overreact. Then Gabe would never trust her with
Mandy.

Erica had already given the child some liquid pain-
killer the nurse had provided before Erica left the
doctor's office, so there wasn't anything else to be
done except to try to keep Mandy as comfortable as
possible. The baby book had a full chapter devoted to
the problem, and Erica had read it as soon as she ar-

rived home. She wanted to read it again now, just to reassure herself, but Mandy demanded all her attention.

The buzzer sounded on the clothes dryer, alerting Erica that Mandy's diapers were dry, but she ignored its summons. Believing a change of scenery might help, she walked out into the backyard and tried to interest Mandy in the bright red roses that grew along the split-rail fence behind the house.

Mandy wasn't impressed. She just went on crying. And Erica kept on walking.

As the medicine began to work, Mandy quieted enough to drink most of a bottle of formula, but all attempts to lay her in her crib proved to be exercises in futility.

Finally, in desperation, Erica returned to the darkened nursery and sat in the antique rocker, holding Mandy close against her shoulder as she rocked and sang and sang and rocked. Slowly Mandy began to relax, her infant sniffles tugging at Erica's heart. Carefully sliding the baby down her body to cradle her in the crook of her arm, Erica sent up a silent prayer that the worst was over.

It was late, later than Gabe had planned on, when he steered his car into the driveway. The porch light wasn't lit and the driveway was dark.

The whole house was dark.

For a moment, just a split second in time, he panicked. But no, Erica's car was in the garage.

Angry with himself for doubting her, he inserted his key in the side door only to realize that it wasn't locked. His heart pounding painfully, he crept into the house, softly calling Erica's name as he made his way through the laundry area to the darkened family room.

Feeling like a dime-store detective, he felt the top of the television set. It was only eleven o'clock, but the television was stone cold. She hadn't bothered to wait up for him, to hear about his day. She hadn't cared enough to listen to how he had beaten Jim Matthews by sinking a twenty foot birdie putt on the eighteenth hole.

He went into the kitchen, turned on the light, and grabbed a beer from the refrigerator. Erica's catered dinner was still on the table, unopened. "What in the world is going on?" he asked the room, noticing that two half empty bottles of formula stood beside the kitchen sink.

Gabe began to get nervous. Erica never left the bottles standing like that. She always rinsed them immediately. She was a real nut about trying to dig dried formula out of the bottom of the bottles. *As a matter of fact,* he told himself, trying to remain calm, *for a woman who said she wanted nothing to do with the running of the house, she had been doing a darn good imitation of Super Housewife ever since she got here!*

Maybe there had been an emergency. An emergency that had required an ambulance, which would explain why Erica's car was still in the garage. He looked around the kitchen for a note, but there was none.

I had to go play a stupid game of golf! he thought, slamming his fist against his palm as he ran down the hall to the nursery. *Erica's been taking care of Mandy for only two weeks. There was a big difference between playing house and being alone with an infant for the first time. I should have known better than to leave. Oh, my God, if anything has happened to either of them, I'll never forgive—*

He skidded to a halt just inside the nursery, his body shaking so hard he had to hold on to the doorjamb to support himself. His eyes had adjusted to the darkness before he dared to look around the room, but what he saw brought tears of relief to his eyes.

Erica was sitting in the rocking chair, her arms wrapped protectively around her niece who, like her aunt, was sound asleep. Erica's head, tipped to one side against the wicker backing of the chair, looked so uncomfortable, with her neck at an awkward angle, that Gabe winced.

Shaking his head, he walked over to the chair and carefully lifted Mandy out of Erica's arms. The child, her short, dark hair curled damply on her forehead, whimpered and jumped slightly in his arms before settling again as he laid her in the crib.

Closing his eyes, Gabe remembered something he never should have forgotten. Mandy had reacted much this same way last month, after her first baby shot. He had called Dr. Halloran, who had told him he'd have to reduce the dosage for the next shot so that they might avoid giving Mandy another reaction to the vaccine.

Obviously the plan hadn't worked. How could he have forgotten that Mandy was to get her second shot today? Gabe walked back over to the chair to look down at Erica, who was still asleep, her empty arms still forming a cradle for the baby. "You had a rough time of it, sweetheart, didn't you?" he whispered quietly, shaking his head. "I'll bet you called me every name in the book tonight while you were walking our little girl."

Our little girl. Gabe sniffed and shook his head. How long had he been thinking of Mandy as *their* child, *their* little girl? As if he, a rough-around-the-edges struggling artist, could actually believe that the sleek, sophisticated Erica Fletcher could see him as anything but a stumbling block on her road to complete custody of Mandy.

Yet she didn't look like a successful business-woman right now, he told himself, looking down at her. And she hadn't looked like one since her second day in the house—the day she had tried to bribe a supermarket clerk.

She looked warmer now, and softer. She looked more human. More approachable. She looked... vulnerable. Yes, vulnerable.

Bending down, he carefully scooped Erica into his arms and carried her across the hall to his parents' bedroom, to lay her on top of the bedspread. He eased off her shoes, then covered her with a thin blanket that lay at the bottom of the bed.

Moonlight streamed into the room and flowed across her form to tangle in her golden hair. Gabe reached out, lightly stroking the blond locks, reveling in the warmth and weight of it, before lifting her head to pull the pillow out so that it laid on top of the bedspread. He wouldn't want her to be uncomfortable.

It would be easy, so easy, to lie down beside her, to spend the night listening to her soft breathing, to hold her hand as she slept. Swallowing hard, Gabe lowered his head until his lips brushed lightly against her forehead. Then he withdrew, to stand at the bottom of the bed, staring at her like a starving man standing with his nose pressed up against the windowpane of the town bakery.

At last he turned away, heading for the kitchen and the can of beer he'd left on the counter. "I must be crazy," he told himself as he plopped down in front of the television set and picked up the remote control. "I must be crazy—and this is going to be one damn long night!"

Chapter Seven

Erica awoke to the pleasant sound of a pair of robins singing a duet just outside her open window. Opening her eyes, she looked around the room, feeling safe, cozy and entirely at home.

She smiled, slowly stretching so that her arms lifted over her head and her bare toes curled against the hobnail bedspread. She felt good; refreshed, renewed. As a matter of fact, she couldn't remember being this rested in weeks. Not since she had moved in with Gabe and Mandy.

Big, rough-around-the-edges, headstrong, "nice" Gabriel Logan. Dear, adorable Amanda.

The baby!

Sitting bolt upright in the bed, Erica realized that she was still dressed in the same clothes she had worn the day before. Her memory came back to her in one sickening flash and she reached out to grab the alarm clock sitting on the bedside table. She had never set it.

With Mandy in the house, mechanical alarms were redundant. It was almost eleven o'clock.

"Oh, my crimminy, I've overslept!" she exclaimed needlessly, slipping her feet over the side of the bed while already unbuttoning her blouse. Grabbing fresh underwear and a simple lemon-color cotton dress, she ran to the bathroom to shower. Still wet, she struggled into her clothing even as she was brushing her teeth.

In ten minutes she was in the hallway, barefoot and slightly breathless, heading for the kitchen. Gabe had taken care of Mandy, she knew that, but he was doing *her* job. That hadn't been part of their bargain.

What if he told her she was unfit to take custody of her niece? She had overslept, after all, leaving a helpless infant alone to cry in her crib. She stopped dead, a sudden realization hitting her.

"In her crib?" she said out loud, shaking her head. "How did Amanda get into her crib? And how did I wake up in my own bed? Gabe?" She hung her head, mortified. "Gabe," she repeated miserably. "You fell asleep in the rocking chair with Amanda and he carried you to bed. Oh, Lord, you blew it this time, Fletcher. You really blew it big time."

Turning on her heel, she went back down the hallway to check on her niece, but the crib was empty, stripped of its sheets and blanket. "He has been a busy little bee, hasn't he?" she sniped, wishing Gabe hadn't been so darned capable, so darned thorough. "But where's Amanda? It's almost time for her bottle."

She headed for the backyard to see if they were out there, playing together on the grass.

The yard was empty.

By the time she reached the family room, Erica was well past panic—and on her way to frantic. They were gone, both of them, disappeared into thin air, with no note left to explain their absence.

Had Mandy gotten worse during the night? Had she really been ill and not just reacting to her baby shot? "Something's wrong, something's wrong," Erica chanted over and over as she paced back and forth in the family room, running her hands through her hair. "I can feel it. Something's very, very wrong. Oh, God, if anything has happened to Mandy I'll never forgive myself!"

The sound of a car pulling into the driveway sent Erica running for the French doors. It was Gabe. Her pulse raced as he opened the rear door of the car to release Mandy from her infant carrier. She sagged against the doorframe, too weak with relief to go to them, and watched while Gabe walked toward her, Mandy in one arm and a bag of groceries in the other.

Shopping! The man had gone shopping? She was standing here, about to suffer heart failure, and he was walking through the door as if nothing had happened, grinning like the village idiot!

"Look, Mandy," Gabe said pleasantly as he swept by Erica, "Rip Van Fletcher has finally decided to wake up and rejoin the world. Good morning, Erica. Or should I say good afternoon?"

"Ha, ha. Very *un*funny, Mr. Logan. Where have you been?" she asked, her question sounding much more like an accusation.

Gabe sent her an evil smile. "Did you miss us? Oh, oh, you did. I can tell. You missed us. Isn't that sweet? Whom did you miss most, Mandy or me?"

"You're impossible!" Erica fairly screeched, wishing she had taken that karate course at the Philadelphia fitness club she used to attend three days a week. Flipping the man over her shoulder and onto the floor would go a long way toward making her feel better.

"Yeah, I know I'm impossible," Gabe retorted, winking. "But I grow on you."

"I wouldn't bet on it if I were you! Don't you know I've been out of my mind with worry? Give me that child before you drop her."

"I took Mandy to the store with me to buy some cold cuts," he explained at last, still smiling as he promptly handed his niece over into Erica's firm embrace. "And, yes, I passed on the hard salami. I bought turkey breast—one pound, not twelve. They didn't have any of that wheat bread you like, so I bought a loaf of rye. Is that all right with you, knowing how you feel about fiber? Oh, I also picked up some liverwurst. You like liverwurst?"

"Only if they sell it in a long coil, so that I can strangle you with it!" Erica exploded, holding Mandy tightly and showering her with quick kisses.

Gabe frowned and wagged a finger at her. "Now *that* remark wasn't nice."

"*Nice?* Do you have any idea how worried I was? Couldn't you have left a note or something?" She tagged along after him into the kitchen to glare at him while he put the meat away. "Why didn't you wake me this morning? And who told you to carry me to bed last night? You did carry me, didn't you?"

Gabe came out from behind the open refrigerator door to look at Erica. "All these questions, Erica. You sound like a cop. 'Just the facts, ma'am, just the facts.' Calm down, before you hurt yourself."

"Stick your head back in there and get your niece a bottle," Erica commanded through clenched teeth, wondering how she ever could have worried that she might be in love with this exasperating man. "That is, if you remembered to make the formula this morning. I used an extra bottle last night when Mandy seemed hungry."

"Here you go," Gabe said, handing her a fresh bottle. "I made the formula this morning while you were catching up on your beauty sleep."

"Bully for you," she sniped. "I suppose you want me to buy you a medal?"

When Erica reached for the bottle he grabbed her hand, his expression gentle. "Take the chip off your shoulder, sweetheart. It isn't your fault you over-slept. From the way things looked when I got home, you must have put in one hell of an evening. I figured we could pull together on this one. It seemed only fair, considering that you let me out to play with the boys yesterday."

Erica pulled her hand away, fighting sudden tears, to watch as Gabe warmed the bottle. "Oh sure, now you're going to be nice to me," she accused, hating herself but unable to stop the torrent of words. "You just love it that I've made a mess of things, don't you? I was doing so well—you know I was. I tried so hard, so very hard, but just throw one little problem my way, one little complication and I fall apart like a house of cards."

Gabe held out his hand, rubbing his thumb and index finger together. "This, Ms. Fletcher, is the world's smallest violin, and it's—"

"Oh, shut up!" Erica groused, collapsing into a nearby chair.

The bottle was warm enough for Mandy and Gabe handed it to Erica, who took it without saying thank-you. "You know what it is, Erica?" he offered, boosting himself onto the counter to watch as she fed his niece. "You can't stand being imperfect."

"Oh, is that so?" Erica remarked, her emerald eyes narrowed.

"Yes, boss lady, that's so. The Complete Executive has become the Complete Mother. I've watched you around here. This place is spotless, even though you warned me you weren't going to touch it with a ten-foot pole."

"Amanda's surroundings are important to me," Erica explained, refusing to admit that she had done anything even remotely domestic just to please Gabriel Logan. "The house was depressing. And you have to admit, everything looks much better now."

Gabe held up his hands in mock surrender. "Hey, I admit it. I don't know how you did it, but it is better. Still, you've taken on the care of Mandy—and this house—as if they were college courses you're determined to pass. Mandy's diapers are washed within an inch of their lives, then folded so neatly I think you use a ruler. And I'm beginning to think you change her clothing from head to toe every hour on the hour. You're a real Type-A personality, aren't you?"

Erica's lower lip began to tremble as her emotions, already under strain, began to collapse. "You think you know everything, don't you? Well, let me tell you, you couldn't be more wrong," she countered, turning sideways on the chair, away from him.

But Gabe didn't heed the warning signals Erica was trying so hard to send him.

He lazily swung his crossed legs as he leaned his head back against the overhead cabinet and scrutinized her profile from beneath his half-closed eyelids. "Wrong? Oh, yeah? Just look at this place!" He spread his arms, indicating the kitchen. "Come on, Erica, take a good look."

She turned toward him, casting her gaze hurriedly around the room. "It's a kitchen. So what?"

"I'll tell you so what. There are curtains on the window, right? Okay, that's only a little thing, but it's something you've done. The cabinets have all been cleaned out and arranged the way *you* like them. For crying out loud, it took me twenty minutes to find that can of sardines I bought the other day."

"They were packed in oil," Erica pointed out in a small voice. "You shouldn't eat so many of them."

"Your care and feeding of my cholesterol level to one side, I'll continue what I've started, thank you, and save the sardines for later. Next, there's the family room," he pushed on, watching her squirm as she patted Mandy to sleep on her shoulder.

"What about your precious family room?" Erica gritted, rising to carry Mandy to her crib.

Gabe hopped down from the counter to follow her into the hall. "It's too neat! That's what's wrong with it!" he shouted, nearly waking the sleeping baby. "Too damn neat," he repeated quietly after Erica had put Mandy to bed and retraced her steps down the hall.

Erica whirled around to face him, her hands on her hips. Glowering, she raked him from head to toe and back again with her icy emerald glare, then smiled up into his face. "Too damn neat? Why didn't you just say so? I hear and obey, oh, master. I can fix that!"

"Now where the hell are you going?" Gabe asked, racing after her as she ran down the hall to the family room. "Hey! Stop it! Cut that out!"

"Too damn neat, is it?" Erica was saying as she tipped over a pile of golf magazines that she had neatly stacked on an end table. Deliberately tilting a lamp shade back to its previously cockeyed position, she moved on to the couch, quickly removing the throw pillows she had bought to give the dark leather some softening color. "Catch," she said, tossing them over her shoulders at Gabe, who caught two of them in self-defence before the third and fourth hit him squarely on the nose.

"I suppose you don't like the way I've straightened the bookcases either, right?" she inquired, not waiting for an answer. Before Gabe—standing in the middle of the room, his mouth open in shock—could think of a place to put the throw pillows, Erica had emptied two shelves of books onto the floor. "There. Does your precious family room have that 'homey, lived-in' look back now, Mr. Logan? Next stop—the living room!"

"Oh, no, you don't!" Gabe declared, reaching out to grab her by the waist as she went storming by him. Erica struggled, and in a moment the two of them were lying on the couch, Erica caught between the too soft cushions and Gabe's rock-hard body.

She fought his containing arms for a few moments, but finally allowed her head to fall back against the cushions, admitting defeat. Physical defeat. Verbally she had, as the saying goes, not yet begun to fight!

She took a deep breath, then asked, "Do you have the slightest idea what it takes to keep a house neat and clean when you're sharing it with a helpless infant and a sloppy idiot? Well? Do you?''

She could feel Gabe shrug his shoulders. "I didn't ask you to play the happy homemaker," he said at last in his own defense.

"No, you didn't, did you?" Erica responded, staring at the ceiling and remembering the day she tied an old pillowcase to a broom handle to knock down the cobwebs in the corners of the room. "You just ordered me to move in here and prove that I could take care of Amanda. But you issued me another challenge, as well."

Gabe stared at her profile, just inches away from him. "I did?" he asked, surprised. "What challenge was that?"

"It figures. You don't even remember. You said, as I recall, that a person shouldn't ask another person to do a job if he or she couldn't do that same job. You said I wouldn't know if the people I hired were competent if I didn't know what to look for while assessing their performance. You said—"

"My turn." Gabe covered her mouth with his hand for a moment, to gain her attention. "I didn't say all that. As I remember it, during that meeting you never let me string more than ten or twelve words together between attacks on my character. You're making me sound like an executive training manual."

Turning to face him, Erica nodded. "You made me think, Gabe. I'm not talking about F and W, because my father started me in the business almost before I was tall enough to reach a desk. I know almost every job there inside out. Mrs. James, my housekeeper, is certainly competent enough, but she's left over from my parents' days. I don't know the first thing about anything but F and W. How would I ever replace Mrs. James when the time comes, or any of the maids, if I don't know what to look for in housekeepers?"

"*Any* of the maids?" Gabe broke in. "Exactly how rich are you, Erica?"

She shook her head, as if shaking off his question. "Anyway, I decided that as long as I was spending the time here, and considering the sad state of the place when I arrived, I might as well learn about house-keeping while I was learning to take care of Amanda."

"Like I said, a real Type-A personality. But I don't see why you're so angry. You're doing just fine with Mandy. You don't need me to tell you that. The house looks great. You make a great breakfast and lunch. In two weeks you've learned to do what I do, better than I do it, and make it look easy. You even find time to lie in the sun every morning for a half hour. If I were a housewife I'd hate you."

Erica's entire body stiffened as she pulled away from him to press herself against the back of the couch. "You stupid, stupid *man!* Easy? Of course it looks easy—to you! You have no idea of what it takes to be a housewife, do you? And do you know why?"

Gabe grinned impishly, his mustache wobbling as he tried not to laugh out loud. "No, Erica, I don't know why. But I bet you're going to tell me."

The tears were back, stinging her eyes so that she was forced to blink. "Because every night, after I was sure you were asleep, I got up and did the dusting and the folding and the arranging and the formula-making—just so you'd think I was a competent mother. I even started reading cookbooks—*cook-books*—so that I could make us dinner one night. That's *why,* you big, dumb, hairy ape! Now kindly remove your carcass from this damned couch and let me up!''

But Gabe wasn't moving. He lay on the couch, dumbstruck. Erica had done all that, run herself ragged, losing sleep night after night, for him. *For him!* She could have concentrated all her effort on Mandy and then sat around eating bonbons while Mandy napped. But she hadn't. She had gone out of her way to impress him.

Oh, sure, he thought, a satisfying warmth growing in his belly, *she might say that she did it as a form of self-education, but I don't buy it. And she sure didn't do it for Mandy. The kid's only three months old. A lot Mandy cares whether or not there's a couple of dirty dishes in the sink. Oh, no,* he decided, feeling better about himself than he had in some time, *she did it for me.*

"Are you going to let me up now or are you just going to lie here all day, grinning like a hyena?"

Gabe's smile faded. He shifted slightly on the soft couch, turning completely onto his side to face her. "Erica," he said solemnly, "Thank you."

He knows, Erica screamed silently, wanting to run away and hide. *He knows everything. Why couldn't I keep my big, stupid mouth shut?* "Oh, no," she moaned out loud, closing her eyes and turning her head away from him.

She was becoming acutely aware of every inch of his long, lean body pressed against hers. His left hand was pinned beneath her, his right arm draped across her waist. When his lips touched the side of her throat, his soft mustache tickling her, she nearly jumped out of her skin. The sensation was electrifying.

I have to get off this couch, Erica told herself. *I have to get out of here before I completely lose control.*

She took a deep breath and turned her head to face him. It was time to confront him, time to put a little sanity-restoring distance between them before something dangerous happened, something that would change their relationship forever.

If escape was really her objective, the move was a gross tactical error on Erica's part.

Gabe was waiting for her. His warm mouth settled over hers, destroying any protest she might have made, destroying her ability to think. He rolled onto his back, taking her with him, their legs intertwining as his hands came up to cradle her head and her back, one hand working to release her zipper.

Erica cupped the sides of his head in her hands, her fingers lightly stroking his ears, running through his hair. Her mouth opened, drawing him inside, and she held him tightly against her, taking as well as giving. She was on fire everywhere their bodies met, straining to be closer to him. Closer, ever closer.

Suddenly she was on her back, with Gabe leaning down over her, one leg pressed between her slightly parted thighs. Her cotton dress gaped at the bodice now that the back zipper had been lowered and she helped him shrug it down over her shoulders, her already opened bra falling away from her, as well.

"Oh, Erica," Gabe groaned, burying his face between her breasts as she held his head, her own head thrown back, her long blond hair splayed against the cushions as she savored the sensation of his tongue worshiping her flesh. "You're so beautiful, darling. So very beautiful. Stop me, please stop me."

There were many things Erica wanted to hear Gabe say, many things she wanted him to tell her. But at least for now, for this moment, the word "stop" wasn't one of them. She shifted beneath him, wrapping a leg around his, running her bare foot down the length of his calf.

Raising his head, Gabe looked down into her eyes, his own eyes questioning. "Erica?" he whispered, his voice low and hoarse. "Do you know what you're doing? Do you know what you want?"

His eyes were so very blue. Like a deep mountain lake. Erica felt she could swim in them, drown in them. She moistened her suddenly dry lips with the tip of her tongue—and gently pushed him away. "Oh, yes, Gabe. I know what I want," she told him, her smile tremulous as he immediately helped her to her feet. "But I'm going to go to my room now anyway."

The rolling sweep of green parkland gave way to a small stand of willow trees, their drooping branches creating a lacy pattern of the sunlight that filtered through to play on the surface of the stream.

A half dozen ducks glided along on the water, having eaten their fill of the bread crumbs Erica had tossed their way. The grassy banks of the stream were wide and comfortable, the deep grass inviting visitors to lie back and enjoy the scenery.

Mandy lay on her belly on a soft blanket, napping in the shade after her feeding, her little legs tucked up tight beneath her upturned rump. Erica sat nearby on the grass, her knees drawn up beneath her rose-pink skirt. She looked relaxed, youthful and very, very beautiful.

"Our little girl is really out for the count, isn't she?" Gabe's voice was a caress as he looked at Erica, his words flowing gently over her as she smiled down into his eyes. He was lying on his stomach in the grass, the chain of flowers he had jokingly woven as a crown for his head slipping jauntily over one eye.

"Our little girl," Erica repeated, her voice as soft as a sigh. "That sounds wonderful."

"It does have a certain ring to it," Gabe agreed, lifting a hand to run his fingertips down Erica's bare arm. How he loved touching her, loved watching her bloom with his embrace. She was all warmth and softness, with no more hard edges or thorny barriers to keep them apart. Their argument, and the scene in the family room had put an end to that, although he had not pressed her for a complete commitment, keeping their relationship steady at its new level.

The past three days and nights had sped by, with Mandy being on her usual best behavior, for which her devoted uncle would be forever grateful. It had rained all three days, not that he could find it in himself to care about the weather, for he and Erica had stayed inside sharing time with their niece.

They had also shared more kisses, more fevered embraces, and several long heart-to-heart talks, and he knew—they both knew—that soon they would be lovers. It was as inevitable as the sound of Mandy's hungry cries each morning at six. Gabe rolled over onto his back and closed his eyes, reveling in the way his blood warmed at the thought.

"Gabe?" Erica prompted, bending down to look at him. "Don't tell me you're going to sleep."

He snaked out a hand to grab her elbow and pull her, laughing, down onto his chest. "Sleep? What's that? I don't think I remember the word."

"Smart aleck," Erica scolded, stretching out beside him to lay her head on his chest. "Can I help it if you kept me up all night telling me of your exploits in college?"

"Mmm," he mused, rubbing her shoulder as he nuzzled the top of her head, tasting sunshine in her warm hair. "I did, didn't I? But, as I remember it, we did a little more than just talk. Are you complaining?"

"No, of course not," she told him, snuggling closer. "Now, just lie still and try to digest those sandwiches. You ate enough to sink a battleship."

Gabe obeyed her by looking up at the clouds, trying to find shapes in them the way he had as a child. He could remember coming to this same place in the park with his family, he and Gary lying in much the same spot, pointing out horses and soldiers in the clouds that passed by.

The memory brought him comfort, and no pain. He swallowed hard, realizing that although there would always be scars, his open wound of grief over Gary's death had finally healed.

"Do you suppose Mandy's first word will be Dada?" he asked after a long, comfortable silence. "I mean, it usually is, isn't it?"

He felt Erica's head nod. "One of the books I read says it's the easiest sound for a young child to form," she said in a small voice. "Ma-ma comes later, although it's the one word children seem to use whenever they want something."

Gabe stared at a cloud that looked an awful lot like his old English lit professor, right down to the man's bulbous nose. "I'd like it if Mandy called me Daddy. I'd like it a lot. Do you think Gary would mind? I mean," he rushed on, suddenly eager to get it all out, "I'd keep Gary alive for her, telling her stories about her real father and keeping his picture around but—"

"But you feel like her father," Erica finished for him, propping herself on her elbows to look at him, her hair tumbling across her face. "I know. I feel the same way, and I haven't been around Amanda ever since her birth. I always thought being Erica Fletcher, President of F and W, was wonderful. Now I think Mommy is the greatest title in the world. It's funny, isn't it, how one small child can change our lives?"

Gabe took a deep breath and released it slowly. *It's now or never,* he thought, mustering his courage. "Mommies and daddies usually live together—at least in my mind they do. Besides, it's neater that way."

"Yes," Erica agreed quietly, her emerald eyes curiously bright.

"Yes, what?" he asked, wishing his heart would stop pounding so hard in his throat. It was too soon, he was rushing his fences. *But it was all so logical, and so right.* "Yes, as in you agree with the theory? Or, yes, as in you'll 'come live with me and be my love'? I do love you, you know, even when you nag."

"Nag? When do I nag?" Erica questioned, her mind reeling with Gabe's admission of love. *It was too soon, too fast, but it was so perfect!*

"Never. I lied. I just wanted to be sure I had your undivided attention. So, what's it going to be? It could work, Erica. It really could."

"Live together? The three of us?" He watched intently as Erica spoke, her smooth forehead wrinkled into a frown.

"You've almost got it right, Erica," he teased. "I think you might have left out the bit about us getting married first." She also seemed to be ignoring the part where she should be saying "And I love you, too," but he wasn't about to bring that up now. First he had to get her to agree to the marriage.

"*Married.* There's so much to consider, Gabe," she began slowly. "There's F and W, of course, and all my employees. I can't possibly live in Allentown and run a business in Philadelphia. And then there's my house, and I—oh, Gabe, *yes!*"

Chapter Eight

The whole house smelled deliciously of double chocolate fudge layer cake, even if Erica's culinary masterpiece had gone straight from store-bought box to microwave oven, with her only involvement being to add some water, vegetable oil and one fresh egg. The cake even made its own icing while it baked, although Erica's artistic hand had drawn the happy face on the top with the chocolate glaze that had come with the mix.

It was the first cake Erica had ever made. She felt happy, almost deliriously happy with her creation, and with life in general. Never had she felt so needed. Never had she felt so wanted. How different this all was from the way she had grown up.

A beautiful, perfumed mother who floated in and out of her life between hosting charity balls and gracing tennis courts, a father who saw her only as his successor in business, and a younger sister whom she now realized she had never really known at all, had been Erica's only family experience.

She had been no more than a part of a pretty, carefully constructed picture, a paragon who did her best to be accepted. But despite all her efforts to please others, she had never felt she was more than an extension of someone else's idea of herself.

Until now. Now, for the first time in Erica's memory, she had become part of a *real* family. This was what life was all about, she had decided. Gabe working in his office, Mandy asleep in her crib, while she, Erica, held it all together—the wife, the mother, the care-giver.

She stood back from the cake to examine her handiwork, licking a dab of chocolate glaze from her fingertip. She wasn't really a wife, or a mother—at least not legally—but in her heart she had become both. She was in love, really in love, although for some strange reason she had not yet confessed that love to Gabe. But otherwise, she was content, *really* content, for the first time in her life. That life had taken on a fairy-tale quality and initially she had trouble digesting what was happening to her, to all of them. She had feared that she might suddenly wake up to realize that she had been living in a dream.

But those feelings had not passed. Nothing was going to go wrong. It was time to make her total commitment to Gabe.

As she pushed a stray lock of hair back from her face, Erica realized that she was smiling. She just couldn't seem to stop smiling. Had Gabe proposed to her only a little more than twenty-four hours ago? It seemed impossible that she could feel so completely changed in such a short time, so settled.

They had talked long into the night, arranging their wedding, which would be very private, very personal, and working out their plans to legally adopt Mandy. Then, with their arms around each other, they had walked down the hallway to Erica's bedroom, her head snuggled against his shoulder, before he had tenderly kissed her good-night and gone to his own room, making no demands on her.

Lord, how she loved him!

Humming snatches of an old love song she couldn't seem to get out of her head, Erica sliced a thick wedge of the still warm cake and slid it onto a plate before grabbing a fork from the drawer and heading for Gabe's office, eager as any child to show off her accomplishment. Without bothering to knock, she opened the door slightly and held the plate inside the room ahead of her, waving it back and forth enticingly to attract his attention.

"Fee, fie, fo, Jake, I believe I smell a chocolate cake," Gabe intoned seriously, stealing across the room to snatch the plate from her hand.

"Fee, fie, fo, *Jake?* What kind of rhyme is that?" Erica asked, stepping into the room to give him the fork.

Gabe shrugged, his mouth already full of cake. "What do you want from me? I'm an artist, not a poet. Mmm, this is great! What do you do for an encore?"

Erica leaned against the drawing table, feeling rather proud of herself. "Would you believe shrimp cocktail to start, followed by beef Wellington, with fresh strawberries and whipped cream for dessert?"

Swallowing his last bite of cake and then licking the remaining icing from the fork, Gabe tipped his head to one side, as if considering her question. "No, actually, I don't think I would."

"You're too smart for my own good," Erica replied, making a face at him. "Well then, would you believe sliced tomatoes, French fries from the microwave oven and steaks on the grill—with you as chef, of course?"

"Now *that* I believe. Come here, woman, it's been nearly three hours since I've held you. I think I'm showing signs of Erica withdrawal. Even chocolate cake doesn't seem to satisfy this emptiness in my belly." Placing the now bare plate on the file cabinet, Gabe slipped his arms around Erica's waist and pulled her close, to nuzzle his mustache against the base of her throat.

Erica leaned back in his arms, her hands on his shoulders, looking up at him mischievously. "Poor thing. Maybe you ought to lie down for a while," she suggested boldly, her emerald eyes twinkling as she suddenly realized how much she wanted him to take advantage of her spontaneous invitation.

"You mean that, don't you? Oh, Erica, how I love you," Gabe breathed huskily, pulling her closer, his attention centered on her mouth. "Mandy? Where is she?"

"Bathed, fed and sound asleep in her crib for at least another hour," Erica informed him nervously, nibbling at the slight cleft in his chin. *Now, Erica,* she told herself. *Now, before this goes any farther—tell the man you love him!* "Any more questions?"

"Yeah, just one more," Gabe said, reaching up to remove her hands from his shoulders and, taking one hand in his, starting toward the door. "What the hell are we doing standing here?"

They got as far as the hallway outside the kitchen before the phone rang.

"Let it ring," Gabe ordered as Erica detoured into the kitchen, pulling him along behind her.

"It could ring forever and wake Amanda," she pointed out practically. "Besides, it's probably only someone else trying to sell us lakefront land in the Poconos. Did you ever think about getting an unlisted number?"

"I *have* an unlisted number, don't you remember? These companies dial by computer now, so nobody's safe. So, are you going to answer that phone or not? I vote not."

Erica lifted the phone from the receiver and pushed it toward him. "Here, growl into this," she suggested. "Tell whoever it is to go away."

Gabe took the phone from her and held it three inches from his ear. "Joe's Bar and Grill. Sorry, we're closed for the season," he announced brightly before handing the receiver back to Erica. "They must have had the wrong number. Here, hang it up."

Giggling, Erica replaced the phone on the receiver, then looked at it owlishly as it immediately began to ring again. "Oh, for Pete's sake, Gabe. I give up!" she groused, putting the phone to her ear. "Logan residence, may I help you?" she bit out shortly.

"Erica? What the hell's going on there? Who was that idiot on the phone?" Gabe could hear the shouted question on the other side of the room. The voice was angry, male, and it had called her Erica.

"Bob, is that you?" Erica asked, then covered the mouthpiece to whisper, "It's Bob Abernathy, my attorney. I wonder what he wants."

"That makes one of us," Gabe groused, his ardor cooling as his dislike for the unknown Bob Abernathy grew. Hoisting himself up onto the counter, his bare legs swinging inches above the floor, he watched as Erica listened to what the lawyer was saying.

"Merrick and Merrick?" Erica repeated questioningly a few moments later, obviously reacting to something Abernathy had said. "Are you sure? I can't believe this. They're old friends of my father's. Why would they think we're a likely target?"

Gabe's stomach did a small flip. Obviously Abernathy wasn't calling to tell her F and W stock just went up three points.

"Damn it, Bob, that's not true!" Erica yelled into the mouthpiece, then lifted her gaze to the ceiling as if mentally counting to ten. Gabe could almost see the gears turning in her brain. "All right, all right, so it's true. I *have* had a lot on my mind lately. Look, I can't do any good from here. I can be back in Philadelphia by..." She paused to look at her watch. "By nine o'clock this evening. Meet me at my office with all the relevant papers, ready to work all night if necessary. No, I *can't* be any quicker than that!"

The phone hit the receiver with a loud bang and Erica turned her face to the wall, the side of her fist tapping the wall lightly but rhythmically as she repeated, "Damn it, damn it, damn it."

"Erica?"

She flinched as Gabe's hand came down on her shoulder. "Bob called to tell me that F and W has become the target of a hostile takeover bid," she told him. "I've got to go to Philadelphia right away." Her bottom lip began to quiver and she turned to lay her cheek against his chest. "Bob says it's my fault."

"Who the hell does this Abernathy think he is?" Gabe growled, instantly belligerent. "Takeovers have become the American way of doing business. The man's a jackass to blame you. It's not your fault, darling."

Erica sighed, sliding her arms around Gabe's waist, seeking his comfort. "Thanks for being angry for me Gabe but, unfortunately, Bob's right. First there was my overseas trip—even though it was well planned— and then there was Meredith's death. I barely went near F and W for a month after she died. I was just getting back into stride when I found out about Amanda."

"Yes, well, it wasn't as if you were sunning yourself on the Riviera. You had personal problems to settle."

"Board members don't care about personal problems. They only care about the bottom line. An absent boss just isn't good business. Merrick and Merrick got wind of it, and now they're closing in for the kill. They've already got three board members on their side. Damn, I tried to talk my father out of going public, but he wouldn't listen to me. Now two of his oldest friends are trying to take the company away from me."

Gabe cupped the back of her head with his hand, pushing his fingers through her hair, trying to ease her pain. "I'll go to Philadelphia with you."

She pushed herself out of his arms to stand in the center of the room, her arms spread wide. "That's a lovely sentiment, Gabe, but how can you go with me? You have to stay here with Amanda."

Gabe shrugged. "We can stay at your house, I suppose, with your Mrs. James. Mandy's old enough to travel."

Unshed tears burned in Erica's eyes. She'd love having Gabe and Mandy with her, but her more logical self knew it wouldn't work. "I won't even be there most of the time, Gabe. Bob said we may have to fly to New York tomorrow morning, and maybe even Chicago, to try to line up board members and sources of financial support. I'll be on the go with Bob day and night."

She watched as Gabe's eyes narrowed. "I see," he said shortly.

Erica laughed, running a hand through her hair in mingled amusement and exasperation. "Don't tell me you're jealous? For goodness' sake, Gabe, Bob Abernathy is old enough to be my father!"

"But Abernathy can help you, where I would be nothing more than a pleasant but unproductive distraction. Mandy, too, for that matter. I thought we were going to be married." Turning his back to her, he ran a fingertip through the cake icing, slashing the happy face's smile in two.

Why was he doing this to her? He was behaving like a spoiled child whose mother just told him he couldn't go out to play. What about her? She had been about to tell him she loved him, about to make love with him! She was being hurt here, too. Besides, didn't she have enough on her mind without worrying about his bruised ego? "Gabe," she began placatingly, "it won't be for more than a week, or two at the outside. I'll call whenever I can, of course, and—"

"Don't do us any favors, okay, Erica?" Gabe interrupted. "Mandy and I got along without you before—and we can do it again.'' Turning on his heel, he stormed out of the kitchen, leaving her to stare after him, open-mouthed.

Erica spent most of the afternoon with Mandy, fussing over her, taking her for a long walk in the stroller. She even gave her an extra bath because it was such a hot day—and because she loved to cuddle the baby afterward, when she smelled of powder and soap.

She washed all the dirty diapers as well as all the clothes that had been in the hamper. It was probably a futile effort. Mandy would most likely be dressed in nothing more than a diaper and undershirt the entire time Gabe was back in charge. Worrying that he wouldn't be able to find anything in the kitchen cabinets she had reorganized, Erica stacked all the cans of formula on the counter and piled a half dozen clean bibs beside them.

While Mandy napped, Erica packed, taking the time to fold every garment carefully and place tissue paper between each layer, all the while trying desperately to keep her mind blank. Then, because she couldn't seem to help herself, she wrote a long list of suggestions to Gabe, just in case he had forgotten some fine point in the care and feeding of their infant niece.

It was nearly six o'clock when, fresh from her shower, Erica walked into the hallway, her high heels sinking into the thick carpeting. The delicious aroma of steak broiling on the charcoal grill drifted in through the open kitchen window, surprising her. She had forgotten all about dinner.

Tentatively poking her head through the open doorway, she saw Gabe reading the directions on the back of a large box of microwavable French fries. He looked the same as he always did, dressed in tan shorts and a navy pullover, his bare feet spread slightly apart as he stood in the middle of the kitchen—looking as at home in that room as a fish would in a parking lot.

Lord, how she loved him! It was tearing her apart to have to leave him. To have to leave Mandy. But she had to go. Surely, now that he'd had a chance to think about it, Gabe could see that? It had been wonderful pretending they were the only three people in the world, locking themselves away in this house, loving each other.

But the world wasn't a fairyland, and it revolved with rules of its own. One of its rules, Erica had learned, was that a person always had to pay the piper. She had been deluding herself—they had both been deluding themselves—thinking that the world couldn't touch them.

It had been the world, and death, one of its sadder realities, that had brought them together in the first place. Now another reality was temporarily taking them away from each other—the reality of the work-aday world, and the business of making a living. Somehow, in the next hour, she had to make him understand that.

"Those, uh, those steaks sure smell good," she offered, slowly walking into the kitchen, her high heels clicking on the tile floor. "I hadn't even realized I was hungry."

Gabe turned to look at her, his gaze traveling from her tightly drawn-back blond hair, past her dress-for-success dark business suit, to her navy-blue-leather-clad feet, and back up again.

His eyes, when they once again looked into hers, were bleak. "I had forgotten how the real Erica Fletcher looks. How the hell had I forgotten?" he said, his voice low and defeated, as if he were talking to himself.

Erica felt as if a knife had just been plunged into her heart. Maybe her fears hadn't been ill-founded. Maybe they had been trying to live a fairy tale. Putting out a hand to him, she pleaded, "Please, Gabe, darling, you're scaring me. Please, don't do this. Please, I'm begging you, don't do this to us."

His dark head lifted as he thrust out his chin belligerently. "Do what to us, Erica?" he questioned her, his voice cold. "I don't know what you're talking about. I'm not doing anything to us. Fun's fun, and all that, but now playtime's over, right, and it's business as usual for the head honcho of good old F and W. I think I knew it all along. We were just kidding ourselves. You don't have to hit me over the head with it. I get the picture."

"In a pig's eye, you do!" Erica was goaded into yelling, raising her voice in the same way she had earlier in their relationship. "You don't *get* anything. How can you be so selfish?"

"Selfish? *Selfish!*" Gabe shouted back at her, slamming the box of French fries onto the counter so that he could dig his fists into his narrow hips. "What the hell are you talking about?"

"Selfish," Erica repeated, standing toe to toe with him, her own hands drawn into tight fists. "You and I are two people, Gabe—*two people*. F and W employs two hundred and twelve people—*two hundred and twelve people* who depend on me for their jobs. It would be lovely to live only for myself, never taking a chance, never sticking my neck out. But I have other people to consider, other people to worry about—''

"Hold it, lady," Gabe interjected, holding up his hands to stop her torrent of words. "Back up a minute there, will you? Just what do you mean by that? Who never stuck his neck out?''

Erica looked away from him, realizing what she had said and wishing she could call back the words. "I didn't mean anything, Gabe." She rubbed a hand across her forehead. "I'm just upset. I didn't know what I was saying."

Slowly shaking his head, Gabe said menacingly, "Oh, no, you don't. You're not going to get away so smoothly this time. You were talking about me, weren't you? You think I'm taking the easy way out, don't you? You think I used Gary's Olympic chance as an excuse not to take my own chances as an artist. You think I even used his death as an excuse to crawl back to drawing illustrations for biology textbooks, so that I wouldn't have to expose myself to the world. So that I wouldn't have to compete."

Erica pressed her fingertips against her throbbing temples. How had they gotten onto this subject? It was the wrong time, the wrong place, for such a discussion. She didn't need this, not now. "I didn't say that, Gabe. Don't put words in my mouth."

"I don't have to put words in your mouth, *darling,*" Gabe responded, his harsh voice cutting deeply into her. "You do a great job of putting them there yourself. I just wasn't listening to you before, was I? You kept trying to pump me about my sketches, my oils, about my single small professional showing. I thought you were interested because...because you loved me. But then I'm the only one who has mentioned that word, aren't I? I forgot who I was talking to, didn't I? How could I forget who you are—the great Erica Fletcher, the be-all and end-all of the art and antique world. Damn it! What a class-A jerk I am!''

Erica reached out, grabbing his arm. "I do love you, Gabe," she told him passionately. "I love you with all my heart. You and Amanda both."

"I've been waiting for you to say that, Erica, but I don't want to hear it now." He brushed off her hand, whirling to face her once more. "And another thing. Her name is *Mandy,* damn it! Why can't you call her Mandy? Isn't it high class enough for you, lady? Just like I'm not high class enough for you? You've been poking and prodding and rearranging ever since you got here. You've been trying to mold us both into something we're not."

Suddenly Erica was very, very angry. She had spoken out of turn, she knew that, and she had been thinking pretty much what Gabe had accused her of thinking—but not for the reasons he had said. She wanted only what was best for Gabe, what his talent deserved.

"How dare you!" she exploded, stepping in front of him. "You are immensely talented, a total idiot, but immensely talented. How dare you sell yourself short? How dare you sell Amanda short—sell *me* short?"

"Nobody could ever sell you short, Erica," Gabe said bitingly. "You cost too damn much."

She longed to hit him, repeatedly, pounding on his broad chest until, somehow, she succeeded in knocking some sense into his thick head. How had she ever thought things could work out for them? She must have been crazy.

"It's no use talking to you," she said, throwing up her hands in defeat. "I have to finish packing—and then I'm going to get the hell out of here!" She whirled on her heels and headed out of the room, calling back over her shoulder, "And your damn steaks are burning!"

The metal lid on the kitchen garbage came down with a dull thud over the burned steaks. Gabe walked over to the counter to pick up the now soggy box of French fries and then consigned it to a similar fate. He wasn't hungry anyway. He doubted if he'd ever be hungry again.

What was the matter with him? He was acting like a selfish, spoiled child. He leaned on the counter and lowered his head into his hands, trying to find some sense in the craziness that had gone on in this same room only a half hour earlier. But, he knew, there was no sense in it—not in any of it—there was only the fact that he was scared. So damn scared.

He had fed Mandy and tucked her back into her crib. The child was already sound asleep, oblivious to the crisis building around her. Gabe had handled his chores with the child mechanically, silently marveling at the fact that no matter how torn up a person could be inside, life went on. The clock still ticked; Mandy still needed to be fed and changed.

But one thing was different. Any moment now, the bedroom door down the hall would open and Erica would walk out of his life.

It was already quiet in the house, too quiet. Maybe she had already gone, sneaking out when he was in

with Mandy, not even bothering to say goodbye. Not
that he could blame her; he certainly hadn't given her
any reason to want to be in the same room with him
ever again.

He walked down the hall, determined to give it one
last shot, determined to find a way to reach Erica, to
make her understand that no matter how stupidly he
had acted, he loved her with all his heart.

Her room was empty. Lingering traces of Erica's
perfume assaulted his senses. The bed seemed to mock
him, the hobnail bedspread neatly drawn across the
mattress, the small tapestry cushions Erica had bought
positioned precisely at the fold in front of the pillows.
A crystal vase full of butter-yellow daffodils sat on the
bureau, the bright blooms reflecting doublefold in the
mirror. The room was neat, welcoming, and vacant.

Closing his eyes, he collapsed against the doorjamb, his heart falling somewhere in the vicinity of his
feet. *Stupid, stupid fool! You left it too late!* he accused himself silently, cursing himself for being so
pigheaded, so determined not to be the one to give in,
to be the one to say he had been wrong.

Lost in his misery, it took him a few moments to
hear the soft crooning sounds coming from Mandy's
room. His entire body tingling with renewed hope, he
peeked into the small bedroom and saw Erica standing beside the crib, one hand extended over the railing
so that she could stroke Mandy's sleep-flushed cheek.

"I'm going to miss you so much, darling," Erica
was saying, "so very much. You won't forget me while
I'm gone, will you? You're growing so fast, and there
are so many exciting new things happening to you
every day, you might be too busy to think of me. Well,
I won't be gone all that long, I promise. You take care

of that thickheaded uncle of yours for me, won't you?"

Gabe swallowed hard, hearing the tears clogging Erica's voice. He felt like a heel. He'd said that he loved her, yet when itch came to scratch, when she really needed him, needed his understanding and support, he was behaving like a jealous, thickheaded fool.

"Erica," he whispered softly as she stepped away from the crib.

She turned to him, fumbling in her pocket for a tissue to wipe at her tear-drenched eyes. "What do you want now?" she asked, walking past him out of the room. "And don't think you can threaten me with losing custody of Amanda. I'm a damn good mother, and you know it."

Gabe followed her into the family room, where he saw her suitcases stacked beside the door. "I never said you weren't, Erica," he answered quietly.

"And don't you forget it!" Erica shot back, her emotions in turmoil. Saying goodbye to Mandy was the hardest thing she'd ever had to do. The only thing harder would be to say goodbye to Gabe. "I—I have to go now," she said, avoiding his eyes. "The rush-hour traffic should have thinned out by now, I think."

"You haven't eaten dinner," he said, searching for ways to keep her from walking out the door.

"I'll grab something on the road if I get hungry," she assured him, longing to get out of the house before she broke down completely.

Gabe merely nodded, reaching past her to pick up her suitcases and carry them outside to her car. Then, as he stood back on the driveway, he watched Erica fumble with her keys to unlock the car door. He was letting her leave, letting her drive out of his life. He was actually standing back, hugging his pride to him, letting her go. Was he crazy? Was he out of his mind?

"Erica!"

She turned just as she was about to slip behind the wheel, her cheeks wet, her face eloquent with pain. Her eyes begged him not to make this parting any harder than it already was. If he touched her again, if he held her, she'd shatter into a million pieces. "Yes?" she asked hesitantly, her voice unsteady.

"I love you, Erica," Gabe said quietly. "We'll be here, Mandy and me, waiting for you, no matter how long it takes for you to come home. And I promise, I'll think about what you said."

She closed her eyes for a second, biting her bottom lip, then looked at him, all her love for him shining in her tear-bright eyes. "Thank you, Gabe," she answered gratefully. "I promise I'll do some thinking, too. This... this separation might actually be a good thing. It will give us both time to...to think things out rationally, to figure out just what we really want to do. We've been moving pretty fast, you know."

Gabe gave her a cockeyed smile. "We sure were, right up until the moment that guy Abernathy called. Just remember, darling, I know where to find you," he warned her jokingly, wishing he could hold her close just once more, kiss her, love her, just one more time before she left. But that would be wrong. He didn't know why, but he knew he had to keep his distance, for Erica's sake.

"I'll remember," Erica promised, climbing behind the wheel. "And I know where to find you. Take good care of A—of Mandy."

And then, too soon, Erica was gone, and Gabe was alone.

Chapter Nine

Gabe stared accusingly at the telephone that hadn't rung more than twice in the past three long, lonely days—and even longer, lonelier nights.

Maybe the thing was out of order? He snatched up the receiver, only to hear the dial tone mock him with its steady buzz. "Damn modern technology!" he exploded, quickly slamming the receiver down once more. "Where is she?"

He rubbed a weary hand along his jaw, feeling the scratchy stubble of a three-day growth of beard. He hadn't taken the time to shave, slipping into the old ways he'd adopted in the busy months after Mandy's birth now that Erica was gone. There just didn't seem to be any point to it. He was barefoot as he slumped in the chair behind his drawing desk, wearing only an old, nearly indecent pair of cutoff jeans. His brow furrowed as he tried to remember the last time he'd combed his hair.

"Probably after my shower this morning," he mused aloud. His three-minute showers, taken quickly so that he wouldn't miss Erica's phone call when it came, were the only rational thing he'd done in days.

His single trip to the grocery store the day before to replenish Mandy's supply of formula still plagued him, as he was sure Erica had called during his absence. He had to get an answering machine, that's what he had to do. But how could he do that? If he left to go to the mall to buy one, Erica might call.

"You're a mess," he informed himself, shaking his head in mingled self-pity and disgust. "I'm surprised poor little Mandy hasn't taken to screaming blue murder at the sight of you."

Mandy. Gabe thanked his lucky stars for Mandy. Without her to cling to, without her to care for, he would probably have gone crazy by now. What was it about Fletcher women that drove Logan men out of their minds?

Gabe stared down at the sheet of drawing paper he had taped to the table two hours earlier. Instead of showing a detailed, cutaway view of the human foot, the page was covered with doodles.

A sketch of Erica holding Mandy was in the upper left-hand corner. Several head sketches of Erica filled the center of the page. He'd captured her smiling, frowning intently, or staring into space, a dreamy expression on her face. Two names, his and hers, twined together gracefully along the bottom margin, tiny rosebuds clinging to the sweeps and curls that held them together. "Logan," he said, grimacing, "you're beyond help!"

Crumpling the paper, Gabe threw it in the general direction of the trash can. It hit somewhere to the left of the overflowing container, to join the dozen or so other discarded papers that were the sum total of his work since Erica's departure.

It was no use, he decided, rising to leave the room, firmly closing the door behind him. He wouldn't get any work done today. He couldn't concentrate on anything but Erica.

Walking down the hall, he reluctantly went into the kitchen, wincing at the sight that met him there. The place looked as if it had been the target of particularly messy vandals.

Dirty pots and pans of varying sizes littered the stove, each sporting a burned circle of grease where he had fried a hamburger for himself—the last one made in the top of a double boiler, as he had managed to run out of clean frying pans.

The double sink overflowed with dirty dishes and baby bottles, the latter all showing traces of leftover formula, a sight that would have angered the fastidious Erica to no end. Gabe had bought prepackaged formula yesterday and a supply of disposable nipples—not caring about the extra cost—but if he didn't soak Mandy's regular bottles soon he'd have to either throw them away or hire sandblasting equipment to clean them.

The thought of tackling the messy job totally defeated him, so he left the kitchen—and the mess—behind him to check on his niece. Tiptoeing into her darkened bedroom, he smiled tenderly as he saw her lying in her crib, belly down, her legs crossed tightly, and her tiny backside stuck into the air.

Her full bottom lip was thrust out and her mouth was making a sucking motion, signaling him that it would soon be time for her feeding. Fighting the impulse to wake her up so that he would have some company, Gabe tiptoed out of the room and headed for the backyard.

The lawn needed to be mowed. Clover flowers dotted the lawn in several places, attracting bees. He couldn't put Mandy on the grass until he'd run the power mower over it. "That's what you get for fertilizing it, you jerk," he berated himself. "The damn stuff grows twice as fast now. You'll have to put some weed killer down now and some more grass seed."

He walked back into the house, letting the screen door slam behind him. "You'll also have to stop talking to yourself, old man, before the little fellas in the white coats come to take you away to the funny farm to weave baskets."

Wandering into the family room, Gabe collapsed his long frame onto the couch, placing his hands on his spread knees that jutted toward the ceiling as his body slowly sank into the too soft cushions. "Gary," he asked his brother, looking heavenward, "what in hell ever possessed you to buy this man-eater?"

He remembered the day he and Erica, in the midst of arguing, had tumbled onto this same couch. A slow smile lifted the corners of his mustache as he relived those precious moments, only to have the smile replaced by a frown as he wondered if he would have to live the rest of his life on memories of Erica.

He slapped his knees with angry hands, wishing he could shut off his mind. Would this godawful day never end? When he had first taken charge of Mandy, Gabe had thought there weren't enough hours in the day to do all that had to be done. Now, with Erica no longer in his life, every day seemed two years long.

How could one obstinate, pigheaded, infuriating, interfering woman turn his entire life upside down this way? How had it happened? When? Why hadn't he been able to see it coming? Or had he been inviting it from the moment they'd first met, encouraging it, hoping for it?

Allowing his head to fall back against the cushions, Gabe closed his eyes, an action that immediately projected an image of Erica onto his eyelids. But when he opened his eyes the image disappeared, leaving behind only the awful, unremitting loneliness.

"God, how I miss her!"

"All right, Bob," Erica said into the telephone, "I'll be ready to go again by three o'clock, but I've got to have a shower after circling O'Hare for two hours. Meet me downstairs in the main lobby in twenty minutes and we'll tackle Abercrombie together over drinks in the cocktail lounge."

Still holding the phone, Erica collapsed tiredly onto the edge of the king-size bed, easing off her high-heel shoes and longing to stretch out full length on the mattress for a quick catnap. "What, Bob? Of course I know Nathaniel drinks like a fish—why do you think I suggested the cocktail lounge in the first place? He wouldn't think of biting the hand that picks up his bar tab. My father taught me how to handle Nathaniel Abercrombie years ago. No, I don't know if it's ethical. Is Merrick and Merrick being ethical? We need his support on this thing, Bob. He has a lot of influence with the other board members."

Replacing the receiver, Erica pushed herself more firmly onto the bed, then laid down and lifted her legs so that her feet touched the wall two feet above the

headboard. Her feet were swollen and her calves
ached. Why was it that every airport gate she'd ever
passed through had been at the wrong end of the ter-
minal? She must have walked forever, dragging her
own luggage, before she finally spotted the uniformed chauffeur holding a card displaying the F and
W corporate emblem above his head.

But now she was here, in Chicago. Three different
cities in three days. She had three sterile hotels, a
dozen exhausting meetings, and at least seven indif-
ferent chef's salads behind her, with at least twice that
many hotels, meetings, and bowls of lettuce ahead of
her. It was enough to bring tears of frustration to her
eyes.

She could only hope her meeting with Nathaniel
Abercrombie would go better than her last meeting in
Baltimore. Mrs. Haverley hadn't exactly been sym-
pathetic to Erica's explanation of "personal problems" keeping her away from the office.

Grumbling about "jet-setting playgirls like you and
your sister," the old woman had insisted on serving tea
in her stuffy, antimacassar-covered parlor. Erica had
graciously sipped her tea and held her tongue, but not
without effort. In fact, gray-haired Mrs. Haverley
hadn't known how close she had come to ending up
with her handmade tea cozy pulled down over her
ears.

Bob Abernathy, loudly clearing his throat several
times and sending easily read warnings with his eyes,
had covered for Erica's silences, and if they hadn't
succeeded in swaying Mrs. Haverley's vote, they had
at least gotten out of the state of Maryland without
first having to bail Erica out of the local slammer.

Lifting her left arm, Erica tried to focus on the hands of the gold and diamond watch spanning her slim wrist. Two-thirty. That would make it three-thirty in Pennsylvania. Mandy should have finished her bottle and be sound asleep in her crib by now, with Gabe back in his office, hard at work. He was behind on his deadline, she knew, smiling slightly as she remembered that Gabe had been too busy with her to work during those last few days they had shared.

Swinging her legs back down to the mattress, she sat up and reached for the phone, her hand stilling on the cool instrument as she hesitated, thinking. Maybe she shouldn't bother him. She frowned, trying not to put her own needs above his need to work. After all, hadn't she been so busy that first day that she hadn't gotten near a phone until after midnight, too late to call him?

She had tried calling him the day before around the same time, but the phone had rung on unanswered for two minutes, more than enough time for him to have gathered Mandy up from her blanket and come inside. After that she had three meetings to attend, without a spare minute to call again.

She pulled a face—the same wrinkled face her mother had ruthlessly informed her bridge club was the reason for her eldest daughter's hated childhood nickname, Monkey-puss. Who was Erica kidding? It wasn't that she couldn't have made time to call Gabe. What about that two hour layover in Pittsburgh this morning? She could have called him a dozen times instead of spending the time trying to read a magazine article on a subject she couldn't recall now if her life depended on it.

She just didn't know what to say to him.

And she didn't know what he would say to her.

Resolutely moving her hand from the receiver, Erica rose, stripping off her navy suit as she headed for the bathroom. Maybe she'd be able to think better beneath the shower.

Five minutes later she was back in the bedroom of the suite, her hair tied up in a casual ponytail, a towel loosely wrapped around her still-damp body and no closer to an answer. Again she stared at the telephone, and the telephone stared back at her.

The damn thing seemed to follow her everywhere she went, the telephone's nine push-button eyes openly taunting her, threatening her, condemning her for the coward they both knew she was.

She ignored its silent siren song as she searched her luggage for fresh underwear and pulled on a new pair of panty hose.

She averted her eyes from its censuring leer as she slipped into yet another crisp white blouse and dark suit and stepped into high heels.

She actually believed she could feel it throbbing with a life of its own as she ruthlessly combed her hair into a sleek, no-nonsense twist at the back of her head.

Finally, at ten minutes to three, she picked up her overstuffed attaché case and purposefully headed out of the bedroom into the small living area. She was only ten feet from the door to the hallway when another telephone—Son of Phone was the name her tortured mind quickly attached to it—silently, yet imperiously, beckoned to her from the coffee table.

"This is ridiculous!"

Throwing down her case in defeat, Erica perched herself gingerly on the edge of the sofa cushion, took a single deep, steadying breath, and picked up the re-

ceiver. "Long distance, please," she told the hotel
operator. "Yes, I know I can dial direct. B-but I'd
rather you did it." *That way I'll be less inclined to
hang up before Gabe answers,* she told herself, wishing she didn't feel the need to keep both hands on the
receiver.

Bbbrrrriing!
The telephone was ringing!
The dinner plate Gabe had been washing for the
past five minutes, trying to rid it of some egg yolk that
had hardened into concrete, literally leaped out of his
soapy hands to execute a perfect half gainer back into
the dishpan, splattering his face with suds.
He raced across the width of the kitchen, bubbles
dotting his mustache and eyebrows, hastily wiping his
hands on his shorts. He nearly came to grief vaulting
over Mandy's empty infant seat, but he righted himself in time to grab the receiver before the telephone
had completed its second full ring.
"Erica!" he shouted into the mouthpiece, not caring that he'd answered the phone the same way two
days earlier, only to find that he was talking to a cem-
etery plot salesman named Bruce.
"Gabe? Is that you? Is everything all right? You
sound strange."
It *was* Erica! Gabe collapsed against the wall, his
heart pounding, his knees shaking.
"Gabe?" There was concern now in Erica's voice.
Concern and a hint of fear. "Is it Mandy? Is Amanda
all right? Oh, I knew I should have called sooner. I just
knew it. Gabe? Answer me!"
Suddenly Gabe was laughing. He had waited so long
to hear Erica's voice again, and now that she was on

the other end of the phone line all he could do was say a silent prayer of thanks and try to recover his breath.

"Is that laughter I'm hearing? Gabriel Logan," Erica questioned, her voice no longer tentative, but stern, "are you laughing at me?"

"Who, me?" Gabe choked out. "Why would I be laughing at you? A person would have to be out of his mind to laugh at you."

"I rest my case, darling," Erica responded archly, but Gabe could hear the relief in her voice, and the absence of nervousness.

"I miss you," he said quietly, sliding his bare back down the kitchen wall to sit on the cool tile floor, his long legs stretched out in front of him. *It was all right. Everything was all right.*

"I miss you, too," he heard Erica say on a sigh. "You and Mandy both. How is everything there?"

Gabe looked around the kitchen, seeing the dirty pots, now full of hot water, lined up on the counters like drunken soldiers and eyeing the sinkful of rapidly disappearing bubbles. He'd been working non-stop in the room for nearly an hour, and the place still looked like something out of Neil Simon's *The Odd Couple.* All that was needed to complete the scene was the character of Felix Unger, standing over him, a disapproving frown on his face.

"Hey, what could be wrong?" he asked, rushing his words. "I'm back in the saddle again, as it were, and this place is running like a well-oiled machine. Did I mix metaphors there? Mandy's fine—fat and happy— and I'm holding up like a big boy. But I meant it when I said I miss you. We both miss you, sweetheart," he added, unable to keep the longing out of his voice. "How's Philadelphia?"

"I haven't the faintest idea," Erica answered brightly—too brightly Gabe thought. "I haven't seen it since late Tuesday night. Bob met me at the house and we drove straight to the airport. I'm in Chicago now, with stops in Baltimore and New York behind me. As a matter of fact, I'm late for a meeting now."

He ignored her hint. "Any success, or are the bad guys still winning?" He wanted to keep her talking, he had to keep her talking. He couldn't let her hang up now.

There was a short silence during which Gabe was sure Erica was deciding whether or not to tell him the truth. At last she said, "It's really too soon to tell, darling. I've lined up some support, mostly old friends of my father's, but there are still a lot of maybes out there. Th—this might take a while, I'm afraid. Maybe another eight to ten days."

Gabe's cheer was deliberate, and he crossed his fingers, hoping his upbeat tone didn't sound forced. "Hey, no problem. Mandy and I are managing just fine on our own. You just go out there and knock 'em dead, okay?"

"Oh . . . okay, Gabe," Erica repeated slowly. "Oh, hold on, Gabe, somebody's knocking at my door." She was gone for a few moments, and he could hear her talking to someone, some male someone. "Gabe? You still there?" she said a moment later.

"Still here, Erica," he told her, his cheeks beginning to hurt from keeping a smile plastered on his face. "Was that Abernathy?"

"Yes, I told you I was late for a meeting. Bob came to get me before our local board member, Nathaniel Abercrombie, slips too deeply into his martini. I—I have to go now. You'll kiss Mandy for me, won't you?''

Gabe nodded, unable to trust his voice. "Yes, yes, Erica, of course I will," he agreed quickly. "And you, too. You take care of yourself, all right? Remember your fiber and everything."

"I promise." Erica's voice was low, so low he could barely hear it. It was as if she had already broken the connection.

"I love you, Erica," he told her softly, a two-handed death grip on the receiver.

"All right, Bob, I'm coming! For goodness' sake, don't be such an old woman. Abercrombie isn't going anywhere without us. I'm sorry, Gabe, Bob was talking in my other ear and I couldn't catch what you just said. Could you repeat it, please?"

Gabe closed his eyes, allowing the pain to wash over him like a tubful of tepid water. "It was nothing, darling, nothing important. I was just wondering where you put Mandy's spare pair of diaper pins. I'm sure I'll find them. You just take care of yourself, and phone me again when you can. Goodbye."

Gabe got up to replace the receiver, then stood staring at the telephone, as if considering whether or not he would feel better if he ripped the damn thing from the wall and drop-kicked it through the kitchen window. He fought down the urge.

"What an ass you are, Logan," he berated himself, stomping back across the room to plunge his hands into the dishwater. "What a complete, absolute, bell-ringing, card-carrying *ass!*"

He picked up the plate he had been washing before the telephone rang, disappointed to see that the egg yolk had melted away on its own. He needed to attack something, even scrub something. "Where are Mandy's spare diaper pins? Don't forget to eat your fiber," he repeated, singsong. "Damn! How stupid can you get?"

Automatically he reached for another dirty dish. "Three days you've waited to hear from her. *Three days!* And all you can do is ask her about some stupid diaper pins? And that guy Abernathy—I don't care how old he is, I'd just like to meet up with that joker in a dark alley some day. Where does he get off, ordering Erica around like that? Arrogant bastard!"

He shook the soapsuds from his hands and headed for the refrigerator, yanking open the door to pull out a cold beer. It was the last one, and he had been saving it for the Phillies game that was to be shown on television that evening. But now he didn't care.

Pulling off the tab top, he watched impassively as the foamy liquid bubbled up to pour over the lid and down onto the floor. He quit the kitchen, leaving the dirty dishes behind, and went down the hall to the family room, to drink his beer and nurse his wounds.

Had Erica really missed him? He thought back over their conversation, trying to reconstruct her words, interpret her tone. He nodded. Yes, she had really missed him. "Sure," he said out loud. "She missed you so much it took her three days to find a telephone. They probably have at least three or four of the things in a place like Chicago. How hard could it have been?"

He sat slumped forward on the chair, holding the cold can against his forehead. How did she feel about him, about the two of them, now that she was back in her own world, away from him? She had seemed to enjoy playing house, if he could use that term, but did it all seem silly to her now? Silly, and maybe just a bit too romantic and farfetched to really be true? Did he really believe Erica Fletcher loved him? Wanted to marry him?

After all, what did he really have to offer a woman like Erica? He was a nobody, a man who hid behind his technical drawings and his excuses for never really trying to prove himself as an artist.

Oh yes, he had understood immediately what she had been saying that last day. If he hadn't been feeling guilty all these years, maybe he wouldn't have caught on quite so soon, but Erica's outburst had brought it all out into the open, where he had to examine it.

And he *had* examined it, much to his disgust. He admitted now that he had been more than happy to drop his art career when his father died in order to help Gary with his dream to be in the Olympics. Although it may have seemed heroic, it had been the easy way out, a way to avoid the pain of failure if his professors were wrong, and he really wasn't all that talented. He could have gotten a job and still kept up with his painting nights and weekends.

"But you didn't," he said aloud, staring at the floor. "And when your first showing dropped like a bomb six months ago and Gary died, you ran straight for a safe bolt hole again, didn't you? What a man you are, what a great big man you are. You have a hell of a nerve asking a woman like Erica Fletcher to love you, to give up her life for you. Logan, you're a real prince."

Gabe looked at his hands, hands that held a beer can rather than a paintbrush, hands whose ache to create had been ignored for so many years. Slowly, carefully, he set the can on the end table and stood up, his spine erect, his shoulders thrown back.

He didn't have time to sit around feeling sorry for himself.

He had work to do.

It was well after midnight when Erica returned to her hotel room, Abercrombie's proxy safely tucked in her attaché case. She was exhausted, and more than a little drunk. Abercrombie had insisted she match him drink for drink, and until she could excuse herself from the table to have a private word with their waiter, she had been forced to down four martinis.

She stumbled through the small living area in the dark, then fumbled for the wall switch just inside the bedroom door. The king-size bed beckoned her and she walked toward it like some sort of zombie, slipping out of her shoes, intent on falling asleep before her head hit the pillow, clothes and all.

But it wasn't going to be that easy, for the telephone was also waiting there on the bedside table, and it brought back the memory of her frustrating conversation with Gabe earlier in the day.

He had sounded so happy, so carefree, so willing to have her a thousand miles away from him. And all he had talked about was diaper pins. Diaper pins and fiber! Oh, sure, he had thrown in a couple "I miss you's", but somehow he hadn't been very convincing. And he hadn't mentioned the word *love* once.

"Maybe he's glad I'm gone, but he just wants to let me down slowly. We were rather intense, being locked up together like that in his house and with Mandy's future to consider," she mused, pulling the bed-

spread back a bit farther and sweeping the two com-
plimentary foil-covered chocolate mints from the
pillow.

Two mints. For two people. In a bed that could
comfortably sleep four. What was she doing here, in
a cold, impersonal hotel room, when her heart was still
locked in a sprawling ranch house in Pennsylvania?
She missed Gabe so much, missed Mandy so much. It
wasn't fair. It just wasn't fair.

Erica laid on the bed, her legs drawn up in the fetal
position and cried herself to sleep for the first time
since she was twelve.

Chapter Ten

Sometime after three in the morning Erica had crawled into yet another strange hotel room, stumbled into bed and fallen asleep before her head hit the pillow.

She woke in a panic only a few hours later, frantically grabbing the ringing telephone only to hear an impersonal female voice wishing her a good morning and informing her that it was six-thirty and the temperature today was seventy-two degrees.

"Thank you," Erica mumbled tiredly, her eyes still closed as she fumbled to replace the receiver in its cradle. "If it's Tuesday, this must be Phoenix," she groused, turning onto her side to try to recapture sleep, and the lovely dream that had included a tanned, smiling Gabriel Logan walking toward her across a carpet of dewy green lawn. His narrow hips had been enclosed in his favorite pair of cutoff jeans as his long legs eagerly ate up the space that separated them. He had held Mandy high against his bare chest.

But it wasn't to be. Both sleep and the dream eluded her, even as reality came crashing in to claim her attention. She was in Phoenix, and Gabe was in Pennsylvania. He had Mandy, and she had her work.

It wasn't fair; life wasn't fair. A single tear found its way down her cheek to splash onto the pillow.

She had been gone ten days. It felt like ten years. Yesterday afternoon, after a four-hour meeting in New York with her accountants and Bob Abernathy, she had begun to believe she could see the light at the end of the tunnel. Then, with the arrival of a telegram last night just before she went down to dinner, it began to look like that light just might be coming from an oncoming train.

Merrick and Merrick had succeeded in buying up an almost overwhelming amount of F and W stock. There was only one hope left, and that hope took the form of one Miss Alberta Longacre Livingston of Phoenix, Arizona. Bob had immediately chartered a small jet, and he and Erica had prepared to take their dog and pony show on the road one last time, determined to make Miss Livingston an offer she couldn't refuse.

But now, her energies depleted, and her morale and self-esteem at an all-time low, Erica didn't think she had what it would take to convince Miss Livingston to come over to their side. She was tired, so godawful tired.

The telephone began to ring again and Erica silently cursed Bob Abernathy for being a never-ending nag. The man was twice her age. Didn't he ever get tired? She snaked out a hand and yanked the receiver toward her ear. "Damn it, Bob, I know what time it is. I'll be there when I get there!" she barked into the mouthpiece.

"And a cheery good morning to you, too," came an amused male voice that instantly had Erica sitting up in the bed, color staining her pale cheeks.

"Gabe! Is that you? How? I mean, hello. No, I don't mean hello. I mean how? How did you know where I am? How did you get this number?"

Gabe's laughter came to her over the wires, warming the pit of her stomach. "I called your hotel in New York and they told me you'd checked out, so I simply went to Plan B. I called Abernathy's wife and told her Mandy was ill and I needed to get in touch with you."

"Amanda's ill?" Erica hopped out of bed, the phone still pressed to her ear. "Oh, my poor baby! What is it? What's wrong? Did you call the doctor? What did he say? Has he called in a specialist? I'll catch the first plane to Allentown."

"Calm down, Erica," Gabe commanded, shouting to gain her attention. "Mandy's just fine. I said I told Mrs. Abernathy Mandy was ill—I didn't say she really is sick. She's fine, honest. I know it was a lousy trick, but it was the only thing I could think of to get your whereabouts out of the woman. But I had to call. I didn't like the way you sounded when you phoned me yesterday."

Erica leaned back on the bed, feeling like a rag doll that had just lost all its stuffing. She took a deep breath to calm herself, but it wasn't any good. Her nerves had taken one stretch more than they could bear. Her chin quivered and she began to cry. "Oh, Gabe," she whimpered into the mouthpiece, "what am I doing here? I want to come home."

* * *

Gabe heard Erica's words and felt a real physical pain tear at his heart. She sounded like a little girl who had gone off to summer camp and had just come down with a first-class case of homesickness. "Hey," he said as cheerfully as he could, "you're in the home-stretch, babe, you told me so yourself yesterday. You can't quit now."

There was a long silence broken only by a few heartrending sniffles before he heard Erica speak again. "That was yesterday morning, Gabe, whole light-years away. Today the bad guys are winning. If I can't swing Miss Livingston over to our side it'll all be over but the shouting. And you know what?" she added, her voice breaking. "I don't care. I just flat out don't care anymore. What does it matter anyway?"

Oh, boy, Gabe thought, wincing. *It's even worse than I thought.* "That bad, huh," he commented, wildly searching his brain for something encouraging to say. He wanted more than anything on earth to tell her to come home, to ditch good old F and W once and for all and come home to him, but he knew that would be wrong. Selfish and wrong. "So," he commented dryly, "the great Erica Fletcher is ready to throw in the towel, ready to fold her tent and slink away? I'll have to wake Mandy and tell her that—thanks to her aunt—she can kiss her inheritance goodbye."

"Gabe!"

"What?" He answered shortly, wincing at the wounded disbelief in her voice. "Hey, what do you want from me? *You're* the one who told me my niece owned a part of the business. *You're* the one who went

on and on about her future. I'm only repeating what
you said."

"Merrick and Merrick can't take Amanda's stock
away from her, Gabe," Erica countered, still snif-
fling. "I just won't be running the show anymore."

"And the name F and W will be gone, right? After
what, three generations?" Gabe questioned, pushing
home his point. "Well, if you think you can't cut it,
Erica, maybe it's best you found out now. You can just
stay home and make fudge. That is what this is all
about, isn't it? You don't think you can play in the big
leagues anymore, so you're opting for what you see as
the easy way out, staying home and taking care of
Mandy and me?"

"I want to be with you!" Erica almost screamed
over the wires, her voice hurting Gabe's ear. "Don't
you want that anymore? I thought we were going to be
married and make a family for Mandy."

There, it was out, what they both had worried
about, agonized over, for almost two weeks. It had
been there, standing between them, during every one
of their phone calls. But now it had been said. No
longer could either of them tiptoe around the issue.
And Erica had been the first one to put their thoughts
into words. Gabe felt a huge weight lift from his
shoulders.

"Oh, darling," he crooned, holding the receiver
with both hands, "it's all I want, all I'll ever want. I
love you so much I ache from loving you."

"I love you, too, Gabe, and I'm not afraid to say it.
I want to shout it from the rooftops," Erica told him,
her voice still echoing her confusion. "That's why F
and W just doesn't matter anymore. I thought the

company was the most important thing in the world, but it's only a company. Don't you see? The company can't compare to what I've found with you and Amanda. I'm not opting out—I'm leaving of my own choosing. All I want is to be with you, love you, live my life with you."

"But don't *you* see, darling," Gabe explained, "we're going about it all wrong. You don't have to give up your career to have a husband and family. You want to live *with* me, but you can't live *through* me— or through Mandy. Besides, love isn't an either-or proposition, at least not in my book. I don't want you to look back in ten years and feel like a quitter, like you let Mandy down, or your father, or yourself."

Her tears were back. Gabe could hear Erica crying, soft, trembling sobs that had the power to destroy him. "Erica, darling, please don't cry," he begged, feeling totally helpless. "We've just found out something wonderful. We love each other. We *really* love each other. I know you were worrying that this separation might become permanent. So was I. But what we feel for each other is real. It has to be, or we wouldn't feel so damn lousy."

He heard her laugh through her tears. "Gabe Logan, you're a beast," she said at last. "But I do love you. I love you so much."

"Then go out there and knock 'em dead, okay!" he ordered, lifting his fist to punch the air. "You can do it, darling, I know you can. And when you get back, I'll have a little surprise waiting for you. Sort of a welcome home present."

"A present?" Erica questioned, sniffing. "Did Mandy cut her first tooth?"

Gabe held the receiver away from his ear and stared at it owlishly. "No, darling," he said at last, chuckling. "This gift is a little more personal than that. How much longer is it going to take before you pin Merrick and Merrick's ears back once and for all?"

"I'll be home sometime tomorrow night—win or lose," Erica informed him, the tinge of fear creeping back into her voice. Her words began tumbling over each other. "Oh, Gabe, I don't know. I just don't know if I can pull this thing off. This Miss Livingston is supposed to be a real Tartar and I don't—"

Gabe started tapping his fingernail against the mouthpiece. "What's that, darling?" he yelled. "I can't hear you. Something must be the matter with our connection. Damn phones! I guess I'd better hang up now. I'll put a candle in the window for you. Go get 'em, tiger!"

He quickly replaced the receiver and released a long breath. "Whew!" he said, looking down at Mandy, who was propped in her infant seat in the middle of the family room floor, staring at a spot of sunlight on the carpet. "This care and feeding of executive types is harder than I thought," he told the child, grinning. "I tell you, sweetheart, it was all I could do not to drag out that old chestnut about winning one for the Gipper."

He knelt down on all fours in front of the infant. "But you know what, Mandy? Erica loves me, yes, she does, and she's coming home real soon." He could feel tears stinging his eyes, but he didn't care. Unstrapping the child, he lifted her into his arms and gave her a big kiss. "Mandy, Mommy's coming home!"

* * *

"So, you're the one giving Jules and Jim Merrick hissy fits. Funny, you don't look like you could fight your way out of a wet paper sack. What do you want from me, girlie-girl? I ain't interested in no high-flown speechifying. Just cut to the nitty-gritty. Why should I give you voting rights on my stock?"

Erica looked across the wrought-iron table at a short spitfire of a woman who stood, arms akimbo, blocking out the hot afternoon sun that danced around her form, throwing her small body into relief. It had to be one hundred degrees on the bricked patio, even if the low, sloping roof provided the small spot of shade Erica was hiding in, one hand held above her eyes as she blinked furiously, trying to focus on Alberta Longacre Livingston's tanned, weathered face.

She bit back a smile, longing to say, "Miss Livingston, I presume," while inwardly thinking that if Annie Oakley were alive today, she would look and sound like Alberta Livingston. "Why not, ma'am?" she countered cheekily, raising her aristocratic chin a notch. "One eastern greenhorn snake in the grass is as good as another, isn't it? And at least you could whup me in a fair fight!"

Alberta Livingston threw back her head and laughed, the sound deep and content, as if it had come from way down low, building in her belly and then erupting, volcanolike, to the surface. "Girlie, I'll say this for you. You've got my attention. Now let's get inside out of this inferno. I had you put out here just because I wanted to see how long it took till you wilted. But you're like cactus, prickly and ready to stand tall all day. I like that. Follow me. We'll grab us a drink and then talk a spell. And remember, just keep it simple. I don't cotton to those high-flown speeches.''

Erica sat back against the uncomfortable wrought-iron chair, shocked at her own temerity, and looked over to where Bob Abernathy stood in his dark three-piece business suit, his tie jammed up tight to his Adam's apple, beads of sweat freely pouring down his face and into his starched collar. ''Bob?'' she asked sweetly, enjoying the incredulous look on his face. ''Want to go inside and maybe get a snort of red-eye?''

Three hours later, Alberta Livingston's proxy firmly locked in her attaché case, Erica settled into her airplane seat and turned to her lawyer. ''We did it, Bob. We damn near killed ourselves in the process, but we did it. All that's left now is the meeting tomorrow in New York and we're home free.''

''*You* did it, Erica,'' Bob told her firmly. ''You had that old lady eating out of your hand. If there's any credit to be handed out here, it's all yours. Your father would have been proud of you. You were magnificent!''

Erica turned to look out the window as the plane rose above the runway and headed east. A small smile lit her features, a smile that quickly turned into a face-splitting grin. ''Yeah, I did do it, didn't I? How about that!''

The entire house was immaculate. Mandy was bathed, fed and sound asleep in her crib, hopefully for the night. A pair of inch-thick steaks were marinating in a shallow dish in the refrigerator. A bottle of champagne was on ice. The salad lacked only the dressing, which sat beside it on the shelf. Two large, well-scrubbed potatoes, rubbed with butter and wrapped in aluminum foil, were already sitting on a table beside the gas grill that would be turned on the minute Gabe heard Erica's car turn into the driveway. Mandy, who had seemed to sense her uncle's nervousness and politely been on her best behavior all day, would nevertheless be awake in less than an hour for her own dinner.

He made one last check of his office, adjusting the corner of one canvas, then backed out of the room to enter it again, trying to see it through Erica's eyes. He took a deep breath, then let it out slowly. She was going to like them, he was sure she was going to like them. *Dear Lord,* he prayed silently, *please let her like them.*

A phone call to Mrs. Abernathy had told him all that he needed to know. Erica had won Miss Livingston over to her side and all that was left was the shouting—in the form of a final meeting that afternoon. If he had figured it right, Erica should be walking in the door in—he lifted his arm to check his wristwatch—*twenty minutes!*

Gabe glanced down at himself, already knowing that he looked a mess. He had left himself just enough time to hit the shower. Turning on his heels, he sprinted barefoot down the hallway to his bedroom.

He had to hurry. Erica was on her way home.

Erica was still riding the crest of a natural high. Her meeting that afternoon had been a rousing success, firmly establishing her as the life force behind F and W, not because of her name or her father, but through her own abilities and due to her own merits. She had, as the saying goes, *arrived*. And, she admitted to herself silently as Bob Abernathy and the board congratulated her at the close of the meeting, she had loved every minute of it.

How could she ever have thought she could give it all up, throw it all away? She must have been temporarily out of her mind. As she steered her car along the highway cutting through Allentown, she fed a cassette into the tape-player, and she soon found herself singing along with a rousing rendition of "Before The Parade Passes By" from *Hello, Dolly*. She felt more than good. She felt great!

Bless Gabe for having goaded her into continuing the fight! Sobering slightly, she realized that he had taken an awful chance, mentioning Amanda's inheritance. After all, hadn't their first terrible arguments been about the Fletcher money? Money, and his motives for keeping his niece?

But Gabe had given her more than a challenge. He had seen what she had not seen. Loving him, loving Amanda, did not mean an end to her career, the career she also loved. He was willing to share her with the world, so that her own life could be complete.

As she turned off the highway and onto Hamilton Boulevard, Erica's smile faded slightly, for she remembered her plan to surprise Gabe by arranging a showing of his art in a gallery in Philadelphia. The thought embarrassed her now. Back then she hadn't been able to accept him for what he was. Yet all along he had gone out of his way to accept *her* as she was. The realization was humbling.

Her hands tightly gripping the steering wheel, she nodded her head once, decisively. "He can spend the rest of his life drawing for textbooks if it makes him happy, or he can devote his full time to his art,'' she announced out loud inside the air-conditioned car. ''As of now, Erica Fletcher is out of the business of arranging other people's lives. As long as Gabe wants me in his life, I'll be there, because I love him for what he is, not what I imagine he could be!''

Putting on the turn signal, she tried to keep her attention on the road as she prepared to turn onto the street that led home. It was just dusk, and she could see a single light burning in the family room as she pulled into the driveway and cut the engine.

Her heart pounding, she walked into the family room, smiling as she saw Mandy's infant seat haphazardly stashed behind the couch, as if Gabe had done a hurried job of cleaning the room. The cushions on the couch were lined up like soldiers at attention, and looked as if they had been plumped by a masculine hand. Obviously Gabe had been busy. She smelled the lingering scent of pine oil in the air.

The house was quiet, and seemed empty. Puzzled, she wandered into the kitchen, expecting to wince at the sight that would undoubtedly meet her there.

But the room was clean, almost spotless. What a change from her first view of this room when dirty dishes had been piled in leaning towers in the sink. Perhaps some of her good habits had rubbed off on Gabe?

Gabe. Where was he? Feeling rather let down at her lack of welcome, Erica continued down the hall to peek in at Mandy. Her heart melting, she tiptoed over to the crib, knelt down and peered between the bars at her niece. Mandy was asleep, smiling slightly as she dreamed her infant dreams, her thumb firmly stuck in her mouth. Her hair was brushed into a finger curl on the top of her head, she smelled of soap and baby oil and powder, and she was dressed in one of her prettiest new dresses. She looked like a princess. Gabe's princess. Her princess.

Their princess.

"Oh, Mandy," Erica whispered fervently, her voice catching as tears stung her eyes. "How I missed you, my sweet baby." She rose, intending to pick up the child, not caring if she woke her, when a slight noise from the hall caught her attention.

"Gabe?" she called softly, leaning around the doorjamb. Then she heard it. The sound of running water. Gabe was in the shower and singing some godawful song having to do with someone having legs and knowing how to use them. Wincing, Erica eased Mandy's door closed and continued down the hallway to the main bathroom.

The door was open, and a trail of discarded clothing led straight to the glass doors of the shower stall. Gabe's body was a flesh-colored outline behind the smoked glass, with only the top of his head visible above the door. His song concluded, he immediately launched into another, one obviously of his own composing, that had something to do with "Er-ic-ca, cha-cha-cha, Er-ic-ca."

Without giving herself time to think, she snatched up a long-handled bath brush and knocked the handle twice against the glass of the shower stall.

The door opened immediately and Gabe, shaking water and shampoo suds from his face and hair like a retriever coming out of a river, stuck out his head.

"Erica!" he shouted, his face immediately reflecting his joy. "What are you doing?"

Erica swallowed hard, her hungry gaze devouring the sight of his bare chest before quickly lowering her lashes to cover her eyes. "Scrub your back, sailor?" she murmured, suddenly nervous, blindly handing him the brush. "I—I'd do almost anything to stop you from singing."

"You could open your eyes and join me," Gabe suggested, laughter in his voice. "That would shut me up in one hell of a hurry!"

"I could, but I think one of us should remain coherent in case Mandy wakes up."

"Mandy?" Gabe's grin widened even farther, if that was possible. "Not 'Amanda'? God, woman, but I love you!"

"I love you, too, Gabe," she answered, turning on her heels and heading for the door. "And just to prove it, I'll start the grill. I'm suddenly very hungry for one of your famous charcoal-broiled steaks. Ta-ta!" She smiled to herself as she closed the bathroom door behind her. She had a feeling he'd be joining her shortly.

"I've carried that picture of my two best girls in my head for two weeks," Gabe said, winking as he shoveled the last bite of steak into his mouth.

Erica sat across the kitchen table from him, the soundly sleeping Mandy cradled in her arms, an empty formula bottle on the tabletop. "Me, too," she said, lifting one of the baby's hands and kissing it. "But, much as I hate to do this, I think it's time I put her down. You will excuse us for a moment, won't you? Oh, I can hardly move! I think I ate too much."

"Maybe you should put Mandy to bed and then take a nice nap," Gabe suggested, his expressive eyebrows waggling welcomingly. "That couch is wide enough for two, remember."

"Please!" she teased as she walked by him. "Not in front of the child!"

"You're putting *the child* to bed," he called after her, leaning back in his chair so that the front two legs came off the floor. "Hurry back, sweetheart. I'll be waiting."

Erica deposited Amanda in her crib, and placed a thin cotton receiving blanket over the baby's legs. As she returned to the kitchen, she suddenly remembered something Gabe had said on the telephone. "Where's my present, darling?" she asked. "If I remember correctly, you promised me a present."

Gabe pushed back his chair and stood up, looking at his most lovable dressed as he was in only cutoff denims. She did notice that, although he had come to the table still dripping wet from his shower—telling her he didn't have time for a towel when his "sexy executive-type" was waiting for him—he seemed to have dried off at last. "I did, but it can wait. Heaven knows I've waited enough years as it is. Now, to get on to another subject, my love. About that couch in the family room—uh-oh, you're blushing!"

"I am not," Erica protested, feeling her cheeks burning with sudden heat. "I'm a grown woman, Gabe. How could you think such a thing?"

"I *think,* my darling, that for all your very wonderful intelligence, you are still as naive as Mandy in some areas. But don't worry, you have me now, and I'll teach you."

Erica gave him a skeptical look. "Oh, really? And where did *you* learn everything?"

"I read a lot," Gabe mumbled, pulling her along toward his office. "But we'll play it your way for now. Come on, and I'll show you my surprise."

"These books you read, Gabe. Did they have pictures by any chance?" Erica teased, holding back as he tugged at her hand, feeling happier than she had in days.

"Brazen woman! They did not! Now, come on, I do have something to show you. I don't think I've slept more than a couple of hours in the past week. Some of this stuff is old, pulled down from the attic, but a couple are new." He stopped just outside the door to his office, placing his hands on her shoulders. "But first you have to promise you'll be perfectly honest about what you're going to see. Okay?"

Recognizing the sudden seriousness of Gabe's tone as well as his earnest, somewhat nervous expression, Erica immediately sobered, nodding her agreement. "I promise," she whispered huskily, crossing her fingers behind her back. "But before we go in there, darling, I have something to say to you, and I want you to listen very closely."

She felt responsible for Gabe's apprehension. Her thoughtless words had goaded him into trying his hand with painting once more, she was sure of it, but that didn't mean he was up to honest criticism, or even that he *wanted* to return to his art. Knowing what she knew now, she wanted to kick herself for ever having accused him of taking the easy way out when faced with the thought of failure. Hadn't she nearly done the same thing, and would have, if it hadn't been for Gabe?

Somehow she had to make him understand that he didn't have to paint in order to hold her love. She needed him to know that she had fallen in love with the caring, compassionate Gabriel Logan, the man who had so willingly and splendidly taken on the role of father to his orphaned niece, the man who had awakened Erica herself to the life and the love she had been missing.

"I don't want you to—" she began hesitantly, only to be cut off as Gabe pulled her into his arms and kissed her with a tenderness that brought tears to her eyes.

"Don't talk, Erica," he said at last, easing her out of his arms to open the door and gently guide her into the room. "Just look."

Erica looked.

She looked for a long time.

She looked at herself as she cradled a sleeping Mandy in her arms, much in the same way as she had just done a few minutes ago in the kitchen.

She looked at a small, freckled, pigtailed child staring at a butterfly perched on the end of her finger.

She stood in front of a small painting of an old man sitting on a park bench, all his worldly belongings stuffed into the battered shopping cart that stood next to him.

She stared for a long time at a painting that showed nothing more than a very young hand confidently tucked in the grip of a very old one.

She caught her breath as she saw the whirling, swirling colors that made up a dedicated young skater cutting gracefully across the ice, a speed-blurred American flag in the background.

Gabriel Logan had given her a present. The most wonderful present in the world. He had given her the present of his art, painted from his soul.

Weeping, loving him, Erica walked into his open arms.

Epilogue

"Oh, no, I'm late, aren't I? If Bob had asked me to sign one more paper I would have cheerfully tossed him out the nearest window!" Erica swooped into the living room, opening the tie of her emerald wool cape and flinging the garment onto a chair so that Mrs. James tut-tutted as she picked it up, smoothing it over her arm.

"Mandy, sweetheart," Erica continued, her voice still breathless, but now soft and loving, "don't you look pretty." She snatched the child up into her arms, kissed both her chubby cheeks, then whirled her once around the room in an impromptu waltz. "Tonight's the big night, Mandy. We're so proud of Daddy, aren't we?"

"Daddy's bye-bye, Mommy!" Amanda chortled, clinging to Erica's shoulders. "Daddy and his funny clothes!"

"She's been very good, ma'am," Mrs. James assured her, winking at the child who had captured her heart three years earlier. "I promised she could stay in her new dress until you got home. Mr. Logan had to go on without you but he said he knows you'll be there as soon as you can. He's wearing his new tuxedo, although I might add that it's strictly under protest. I tied his tie for him after he made a sad botch of it."

"Yes, Mrs. James, I'm sure he did, and thank you so much. That's one of the reasons I wanted to get home early. I'm surprised he didn't strangle himself with it, poor baby," Erica said, remembering the fight Gabe had put up about the tuxedo. She was grateful Mrs. James had helped out.

Kissing Mandy and promising to make her three, count them, *three* Mickey Mouse-shaped pancakes for breakfast, Erica handed the child to the housekeeper, then smiled, knowing Gabe must be beside himself with nerves, even if he had done all this before. "That man," she said to Mrs. James, winking. "He hates these showings. I'll just change my clothes and look in on Matthew and then be on my way to effect a rescue. Has he been good?"

"When is he bad?" Mrs. James asked, sniffing. "Mr. Logan wanted to take him along, he and Mandy both, but I talked him out of it. Honestly, Mrs. Logan, if your husband had his way, those children would never leave his side."

"That's because he's still a child himself, Mrs. James," Erica said with a laugh as she jogged up the long, curving staircase, already unbuttoning the cuffs of her severely tailored silk blouse. Leave it to Gabe! He'd take Mandy and Matthew everywhere, he was that proud of his children. She slowed her pace as she walked down the hall, opening a bedroom door and peeking inside to see her son, sound asleep in his crib. He slept the same way Mandy did, on his belly, his diaper-thick rump pointing at the ceiling.

In the six months since his birth, Erica had still not quite believed that she could be the mother of something so beautifully, wonderfully perfect. Matthew had her green eyes and Gabe's dark hair, he and his sister Mandy looking enough alike to be twins. "I love you, sweet thing," she whispered softly before closing the door.

Fifteen minutes later, Erica was in her car heading downtown, her floor-length gown tucked inelegantly between her knees so that it wouldn't get caught beneath her heels as she drove. Her life was so hectic, so full, but so very, very satisfying. She had a husband she loved, two wonderful children, and a career she could be proud of—what more could a woman ask?

She could ask for a parking space, that's what she could ask for, she thought, having circled the block twice without finding one. At last, just when she was about to take her chances parking in a loading zone, another car pulled away from the curb and she quickly slipped hers into the space. Grabbing up her evening purse, she jogged to the door of the Rawlings Gallery while still hunting for her invitation, thanked the man holding the door open for her and skidded to a halt three feet inside the door.

The hum of earnest conversation surrounded her as she made her way through the crowd, her chin high, a slight smile on her face.

"Isn't it wonderful?" she heard a man saying to his companion. "His work is so alive, so vibrant. I hear Emily Smithers bought three of his paintings at his last show and they've more than doubled in value already."

"I don't care if they triple in value, I wouldn't part with mine," his companion countered. "I tell you, it brings tears to my eyes every time I look at it."

"Look, there's his wife, Erica," a woman said, envy in her voice. "She models for him, you know, although he never sells those paintings. They're very much in love, more's the pity. Not only is he talented, but Gabriel Logan is one handsome son of a—"

"Hello, darling. I've been looking for you," Gabe said, holding out his hand as Erica approached. He looked so uncomfortable, yet so devilishly handsome in his tuxedo that she couldn't wait to get him home and out of it.

Erica took his hand and let him pull her into the circle of his arm. "From the whispers I heard walking over here, you've got another hit on your hands with this showing, Mr. Logan, not that there was a doubt in my mind. Have I ever told you that I'm very, *very* proud to be your wife?" she asked, kissing his cheek.

"Not in the past half hour, no," Gabe responded, grinning at her. "Do you really think they like it?"

"Not only is your work to their liking, darling, but I think I may have to start watching my back. The ladies seem to want the artist as much as they want his art."

Gabe squeezed his wife's slim waist and growled into her ear. "Well, they can't have me. I'm spoken for. How are the kids?"

"Fine," Erica told him, accepting a glass of champagne a uniformed waiter offered. "I broke the news to Bob that we're going away for two months. That's why I'm late. I had to console him."

Gabe laughed out loud. "Two months with just my wife and my two kids. If Abernathy ever found out that we sneak back to Allentown and play house, he'd have a stroke. Where did you tell him we were going this time?"

"Hawaii," Erica said, waving to a friend across the room. "He warned me about getting too much sun. Hey!" She nearly spilled her champagne as Gabe grabbed her free hand and pulled her across the gallery and into a room marked Private.

"Come here, wife, and let's neck," Gabe ordered once he had closed the door behind them. Taking the glass from her hand, he set it on a table so that he could place her hands on his shoulders.

"Gabe!" Erica scolded halfheartedly, loving the look in his eyes as he stared down at her. "You're not supposed to be in the manager's office, seducing your wife. You're supposed to mingle with the critics and customers."

Grinning wickedly, Gabe pulled her tightly against him. "Yeah, how about that?" he murmured, just before his lips met hers, and the world faded away.

* * * * *

**Three All-American beauties discover
love comes in all shapes and sizes!**

ALL-AMERICAN SWEETHEARTS

by Laurie Paige

CARA'S BELOVED (#917)—*February*

SALLY'S BEAU (#923)—*March*

VICTORIA'S CONQUEST (#933)—*April*

A lost love, a new love and a hidden one, three
All-American Sweethearts get their men in Paradise Falls,
West Virginia. Only in America...and only
from Silhouette Romance!

Silhouette
R O M A N C E™

SRLP1

HE'S MORE THAN A MAN, HE'S ONE OF OUR

HAUNTED HUSBAND
Elizabeth August

Thatcher Brant, widower and father of two, was so busy keeping the peace in Smytheshire, Massachusetts, he hadn't time to think about romance. But this chief of police was in for quite an awakening when his childhood nemesis, Samantha Hogan, moved into his house. How could Thatcher have ever guessed that fate would bring Samantha—the woman he had never dared care about—close enough to touch?

Find out if the best things in life truly come to those who wait, in Elizabeth August's HAUNTED HUSBAND, available in March.

Fall in love with our FABULOUS FATHERS—and join the Silhouette Romance family!

**Silhouette Books
is proud to present
our best authors,
their best books...
and the best in
your reading pleasure!**

Throughout 1993, look for exciting books
by these top names in contemporary
romance:

CATHERINE COULTER—
Aftershocks in February

FERN MICHAELS—
Whisper My Name in March

DIANA PALMER—
Heather's Song in March

ELIZABETH LOWELL—
Love Song for a Raven in April

SANDRA BROWN
(previously published under
the pseudonym Erin St. Claire)—
Led Astray in April

LINDA HOWARD—
All That Glitters in May

When it comes to passion,
we wrote the book.

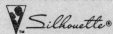

BOBT1R

Take 4 bestselling love stories FREE

Plus get a FREE surprise gift!

For all those readers who've been looking for something a little bit different, a little bit spooky, let Silhouette Books take you on a journey to the dark side of love with

SILHOUETTE Shadows™

If you like your romance mixed with a hint of danger, a taste of something eerie and wild, you'll love Shadows. This new line will send a shiver down your spine and make your heart beat faster. It's full of romance and more—and some of your favorite authors will be featured right from the start. Look for our four launch titles wherever books are sold, because you won't want to miss a single one.

THE LAST CAVALIER—Heather Graham Pozzessere
WHO IS DEBORAH?—Elise Title
STRANGER IN THE MIST—Lee Karr
SWAMP SECRETS—Carla Cassidy

After that, look for two books every month, and prepare to tremble with fear—and passion.

SILHOUETTE SHADOWS, coming your way in March.

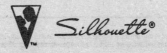

Silhouette®

SHAD1